W9-DIH-604

At Issue

| The BP Oil Spill

Other Books in the At Issue Series:

At Issue

The BP Oil Spill

David Haugen, Book Editor

GREENHAVEN PRESS
A part of Gale, Cengage Learning

Detroit • New York • San Francisco • New Haven, Conn • Waterville, Maine • London

Elizabeth Des Chenes, *Managing Editor*

LIBRARY OF CONGRESS CATALOGING-IN-PUBLICATION DATA

The BP oil spill / David Haugen, book editor.
    p. cm. -- (At issue)
    Includes bibliographical references and index.
    ISBN 978-0-7377-5568-8 (hardcover) -- ISBN 978-0-7377-5569-5 (pbk.)
    1. BP Deepwater Horizon Explosion and Oil Spill, 2010--Juvenile literature. 2. Oil spills--Environmental aspects--Mexico, Gulf of--Juvenile literature. 3. Oil wells--Mexico, Gulf of--Blowouts--Juvenile literature. I. Haugen, David M., 1969-
    TD427.P4.B65 2011
    363.738'20916364--dc23

                                                                    2011023560

Printed in the United States of America
1 2 3 4 5 6 7 15 14 13 12 11

Contents

Introduction

On April 20, 2010, an explosion on the Deepwater Horizon oil rig in the Gulf of Mexico resulted in the deaths of eleven crewmen and a three-month-long oil leak that spread almost 206 million gallons of crude oil throughout nearby coastal waters. The rig, owned by a company called Transocean and leased to British Petroleum (BP), had recently finished drilling an exploratory shaft 5,000 feet below sea level (and another three miles below the earth's surface) when disaster struck. Around ten o'clock that night, a blast of flammable methane gas shot up the main shaft through a broken seal. The gas cloud caught fire and engulfed the rig as workers frantically attempted to escape the blaze by safety boats. The rig platform burned, and stray oil set some of the surrounding water afire. The conflagration did not end until Deepwater Horizon collapsed the following day.

Because the blowout preventer (BOP) at the bottom of the Deepwater Horizon shaft failed to cap the well at the first sign of trouble, a steady gush of oil permeated the waters around the gulf region. BP and government officials initially estimated about 42,000 to 210,000 gallons were leaking from the wellhead each day. In August, that number was revised to over 2,600,000 gallons (or roughly 62,000 barrels) of oil per day. Working with varying local cleanup crews, BP laid devices called flotation booms in the area to contain the surface spread. On April 29, CBS News reported that 685,000 gallons of oil had been scooped up from the polluted waters, but the Coast Guard still expected the oil slick to reach the Louisiana coast. Indeed, despite the use of underwater chemical dispersants and surface burning operations, oil lapped up on Louisiana shores the next day. President Barack Obama pledged national resources to help stem the leak and clean up any damage—though he assured the public that BP would foot the bill. "While BP is ultimately responsible for funding the cost of response and cleanup operations, my administration will continue to use every single available resource at our disposal . . . to address the incident," the President stated in a press conference on that day oil first hit Louisiana. By early June, oil from the spill reached Mississippi, Alabama, and Florida. So many compacted oil blobs made their way to the sands along the far western reach of Florida that a June 3 Associated Press (AP) piece claimed, "Swimmers at Pensacola Beach rushed out of the water after wading into the mess, while other beachgoers inspected the clumps with fascination, some taking pictures. Children were seen playing with the globs as if they were Play-Doh."

On the same day that the AP story ran, BP affixed a cap to a shorn-off piece of the well shaft in hopes of halting the oil flow. The cap failed to secure tightly enough to do the job. Subsequent efforts—including dropping a huge cement dome over the leak at the sea floor—also proved unsuccessful. US Coast Guard Commandant Admiral Thad Allen, the government's liaison and chief official on this operation, was quoted in the *Miami Herald* on May 8 as stating, "We're captives to the tyranny of what I call distant depth, and there is no human access to the site of the spill." It was not until July 13 that robotic submersibles fitted a second cap to the wellhead that staunched the oil leak in a few days. In August, relief wells (which BP had begun drilling in May) reached the site, and BP started pumping a mixture of mud and cement into the original bore hole to permanently seal the leak. Overall, BP announced that by November 2010, the leak and its cleanup would likely cost the company $40 billion.

Part of the expected costs of the disaster was a $20 billion fund set aside to settle claims against the company from gulf coast businesses. Many fisheries, shrimping fleets, and tourist companies asserted that the oil spill had severely crippled their livelihoods after the government closed the waters between the Mississippi River and Pensacola to commercial and recreational business in early May. Since then, however, BP has come under fire for delaying payments. As of February 2011, the fund had only paid out $1.4 billion to individual claimants and $1.9 billion to businesses.

BP is also responsible for ecological damage resulting from the spill. As soon as the leak emerged, environmentalists were concerned about the dire consequences to marine wildlife and birds that nest in coastal regions. Some were fearful that fragile marshlands would be destroyed and that shellfish—which move too slowly to escape the oil—would suffer along the tar-filled sands of area beaches. However, visible damage was minimal even two months after the explosion. On July 5, David A. Fahrenthold wrote a piece for the *Washington Post* that noted only 1,200 birds had been found dead as a result of the spill—a very low number in comparison to the deaths caused by other notable spills. The impact on marshlands was still in dispute, and "Further offshore, federal scientists and university researchers have disagreed about the existence of 'plumes' or 'clouds' of dissolved or submerged oil," Fahrenthold reported. Some optimistic analysts argued that the currents carried much of the oil out to sea where it was widely dispersed and that the sun had evaporated much of the surface slicks. Other researchers suggested the visible damage was no indication of the long-term ecological harm of so much oil in gulf habitats. Fahrenthold quoted Roger Helm, a US Fish and Wildlife Service official, as asserting, "The possibility of having significant changes in the food chain, over some period of time, is very real. The possibility of marshes disappearing . . . is very real."

In the wake of the largest oil spill in US history, the Department of the Interior ordered a moratorium on new drilling operations in the Gulf of Mexico to allow time for government inspections. Several companies fought the ban, and at least one US federal court deemed it arbitrary. Within six months, the moratorium was lifted—the government claimed new safety standards were in place that would prevent another disaster, but environmentalists were not convinced the root causes had been addressed. Then in December 2010, the administration reversed its decision, claiming it was freezing new oil and gas leases for drilling in the Gulf of Mexico and along the Atlantic Coast until 2017. Interior Secretary Ken Salazar said, "We believe the most appropriate course of action is to focus development on areas with existing leases and not expand to new areas at this time." Oil companies continue to fight this new ban, insisting that such a stringent measure will cost America jobs and vital energy resources. Supporters of the ban maintain it will give authorities time to assess the impact of the Deepwater Horizon catastrophe and find ways to avert such disasters in the future.

In *At Issue: The BP Oil Spill*, various experts, analysts, journalists, and pundits give their views on the BP oil spill and the consequences of drilling in the region. Some hope to affix blame and punish those in charge; others hope the lessons of this tragedy will help shape future energy policies. The debate over continued drilling endures even as the presidential ban remains in effect. As President Obama noted in a speech he made about offshore drilling on March 31, 2010—a month before the BP oil spill—the question of how to meet the country's energy needs while respecting ecosystems is difficult but imperative. The President stated, "The answer is not drilling everywhere all the time. But the answer is not, also, for us to ignore the fact that we are going to need vital energy sources to maintain our economic growth and our security." While some maintain that drilling must eventually continue and even expand, others emphasize that America must find alternatives that will ultimately end the nation's search for more fossil fuel.

1

BP Spread the Blame for the Oil Spill to Its Contractors

Steven Mufson and David Hilzenrath

Steven Mufson and David Hilzenrath are staff writers for the financial section of the Washington Post.

In its September 8, 2010 investigation results report, British Petroleum (BP) said the April 20 oil rig blowout and subsequent oil spill had many contributing causes. Chiefly, the company laid the blame at the feet of its contractors who were responsible for a host of structural and equipment failures that facilitated the disaster. Although the named contractors denied their culpability, BP insists it alone cannot be faulted for the accident. Regrettably, the report does not address BP's broader safety policies and standards.

BP rolled out the results Wednesday [September 8, 2010] of a four-month internal investigation into the causes of the April 20 blowout of its Macondo oil well in the Gulf of Mexico, spreading blame among its contractors and giving a glimpse of the defenses it might deploy in public and in court.

The much-anticipated report asserted that a "complex and interlinked series" of failures—of equipment, engineering and judgment—led to the surge of oil and gas that exploded on the deck of the Deepwater Horizon drilling rig, killing 11 people, sinking the rig and triggering the worst oil spill in U.S. history.

The report was written by a team of 50 internal and external experts led by the company's head of safety and operations, Mark Bly, and the rollout Wednesday morning at a hotel in downtown Washington was labeled a "technical briefing."

BP Argues for Shared Responsibility

But the document inevitably carries a heavy public relations element as well as legal and financial implications for BP. It arrives as the Justice Department is weighing whether to bring charges of criminal negligence against BP that could sharply increase the cost of the spill for the London-based oil giant and provide fodder for private lawsuits.

In addition, there is legislation in Congress that would effectively strip BP of the right to drill in the Gulf of Mexico. The company is haggling with the [Barack] Obama administration over what pieces of collateral to offer while it is financing the $20 billion escrow fund that will be used to pay claims. And BP's main partner in the well, Anadarko Petroleum, has declared that it won't pay its share of the cleanup costs and claims because it views BP's well design and actions as reckless.

The BP report makes the case for "shared responsibility," saying that "no single factor" caused the blowout. It points to multiple failures by its contractors in maintenance, equipment and planning.

The report did not say how far up the BP corporate ladder the well problems went, and no employee was named or punished.

The investigation found fault with the recipe Halliburton used in its cement, with the flaps on a Weatherford International barrier device known as a float collar, and with the condition of hydraulic lines and batteries that might have sapped power from the blowout preventer made by Cameron International and operated by Transocean, making it impossible to clamp and cut through steel piping.

"Transocean was solely responsible for operation of the drilling rig and for operations safety," the report says in an appendix. "It was required to maintain well control equipment and use all reasonable means to control and prevent fire and blowouts."

The report also said Transocean and BP rig leaders jointly "reached the incorrect view" on well tests in the crucial hours before the explosion. And Bly said BP needs to reexamine the way it oversees work by its contractors.

BP Stands by Its Well Design

Yet the report absolves BP's widely criticized well design. It says the path that oil and gas followed as they escaped from the well meant that the well's casing and design—matters that could otherwise implicate BP—were not factors in the disaster. Instead, it says that if any one of eight failures of equipment or decision-making had not taken place, the blowout would not have happened.

The report not only offers new details and analysis of what went wrong, it also represents a bold declaration that BP is not going to assume more than what it considers its share of the blame for the accident. The report did not say how far up the BP corporate ladder the well problems went, and no employee was named or punished.

In a news release, BP chief executive Tony Hayward, who has barely spoken publicly since his disastrous congressional testimony in June, did not offer anything resembling a mea culpa.

Instead, Hayward, who has agreed to step down Oct. 1, said, "It is evident that a series of complex events, rather than a single mistake or failure, led to the tragedy." He added, "Multiple parties, including BP, Halliburton and Transocean, were involved."

BP's Contractors Respond

BP's contractors fired back at the company, as did some members of Congress who think BP should shoulder responsibility for the accident and be harshly punished for the damage to the Gulf Coast's environment and economy.

Rep. Edward J. Markey (D-Mass.), a senior member of the House Energy and Commerce Committee, said that "BP is happy to slice up blame, as long as they get the smallest piece."

Transocean, the world's largest operator of deepwater drilling rigs, issued a statement saying, "This is a self-serving report that attempts to conceal the critical factor that set the stage for the Macondo incident: BP's fatally flawed well design." It added: "In both its design and construction, BP made a series of cost-saving decisions that increased risk—in some cases, severely."

BP said that even in the final minutes before the explosion, disaster might have been averted if the gas had been directed off the rig.

Halliburton also decried the report, in which it was faulted for using too much nitrogen in a foamlike cement mixture that BP's team said was "very likely unstable" and that one investigator compared to shaving cream going flat. The report said that Halliburton had not properly tested the cement slurry and that requests for samples from Halliburton were rebuffed. But BP asked an independent lab to create a "representative sample," based on the known design of the cement, and found through its own testing that, as investigator Kent Corsor put it, "The slurry was too thin."

Halliburton replied in a statement that "the well owner is responsible for designing the well program and any testing related to the well. Contractors do not specify well design or make decisions regarding testing procedures as that responsibility lies with the well owner."

Halliburton added that BP's report has "a number of substantial omissions and inaccuracies," but it did not say what those are.

Weatherford declined to comment.

Unaddressed Issues

BP said that even in the final minutes before the explosion, disaster might have been averted if the gas had been directed off the rig. Instead it was sent to a mud gas separator, which vented the gas onto the rig.

One issue that BP's critics have cited has been the company's decision to use only six instead of 21 centralizers, devices for centering the drill pipe in the well.

But the BP report said that there was no evidence of "channeling" by gas above the main oil- and gas-bearing reservoir, and that as a result the decision to go ahead with just six centralizers "likely did not contribute to the cement's failure to isolate the main hydrocarbon zones."

The BP investigatory group, in an effort to avoid internal conflicts, drew on internal drilling experts from places such as Alaska rather than the Gulf of Mexico. The group also brought in outside experts and hired third parties to conduct tests. They drew on interviews with rig workers, e-mails and data transmitted to shore.

But they lacked evidence from inside the blowout preventer, which was lifted from the sea floor Friday and is in government custody.

Though BP officials said the investigation team had been given wide authority and independence, Bly said he briefed executives and board members on several occasions. And the investigation did not address issues of the company's safety culture.

Asked whether the probe overlapped with his area of responsibility, Bly said that he dealt "at a very high level." He said, "You could say that the investigation caused me to investigate things related to me," but "it's a somewhat distant linkage."

He said he does not believe that widely cited pressures to save time and money on the expensive rig were to blame for the disaster. "My view is that we didn't see any indications that support that."

2

America's Dependence on Fossil Fuel Is to Blame for the Oil Spill

Jeremy Hance

Jeremy Hance is a writer for mongabay.com, an environmental website.

The April 20, 2010 oil spill in the Gulf of Mexico should not have been unexpected. After all, big corporations like British Petroleum (BP) continue to drill in pursuit of profits, and Americans seem content to let fossil fuel consumption go unabated. US politicians also encourage drilling to satisfy the economic status quo instead of investing in alternative energies. Perhaps the spill will serve as a wake-up call for the nation, but realistically Americans got the spill they deserved and will probably tolerate the next one because the country has not learned to wean itself off oil and other fossil fuels.

America, we deserve the oil spill now threatening the beautiful coast of Louisiana. This disaster is not natural, like the earthquake that devastated Haiti or tsunami that swept Southeast Asia in 2006; this disaster is man-made, American-made in fact, pure and simple.

So, while in the upcoming weeks and months—if things go poorly—we may decry the oil-drenched wildlife, the economic loss for the region, the spoiled beaches, the wrecked ecosystems, the massive disaster that could take decades if not longer to recover from, we, as Americans, cannot think smugly that we are somehow innocent of what has happened. You play with fire: you will get burned. You drill for oil 1,500 meters below the surface of the ocean, you open up oil holes across the surface of your supposedly beloved landscape, sooner or later there will be a spill, and sometimes that spill will be catastrophic.

Corporations don't really care about environmental protections—unless they are required to—nor do they spend their time deeply fretting over worker safety—unless, again, someone requires they do.

BP Behaved Like Any Other Big Company

We can't blame BP for this disaster: the tragic loss of life or the petroleum miasma now spreading across the gulf. We can't blame them even though they lobbied time and again against tougher regulations—and won—including requiring a remote valve system that may have shut down the spill now occurring. Even though they fought greater and more frequent government oversight—and also won—arguing that voluntary regulations were enough.

We can't blame BP because this is how large corporations act. Big corporations don't make decisions based on ethical considerations, but something they refer to as 'risk assessment', measuring likely outcomes against monetary costs. What is the likelihood of a massive spill that will devastate the Gulf of Mexico? BP thought the level of risk was worth not spending 500,000 US dollars on a remote valve—and instead spent over fifteen million dollars lobbying against such measures. BP did what big companies do: only as much as government requires of them (and sometimes public outcry) and fudges the rest.

After all Americans have endured recently from big corporations—coal ash disaster, financial meltdown, mining deaths—this shouldn't be at all surprising for the public. This, in fact, should be expected. Corporations, especially of multi-billion dollar, multi-national, greenwashing-variety, don't really care about environmental protections—unless they are required to—nor do they spend their time deeply fretting over worker safety—unless, again, someone requires they do.

America's Economy Allows for Such Accidents

Despite all the PR [public relations] money can buy, BP isn't trying to make a better world, only a more profitable one—for its shareholders. It has no other motive, purpose, or goal. This isn't a secret, but considered a cardinal rule from every class of Econ 101 to Wall Street to BP's offices.

We also can't blame President Obama for opening up millions of acres to offshore drilling, because this is what politicians do: they compromise.

One could argue that corporations shouldn't be allowed to act in such a way, but again it's our laws, our regulations (or lack thereof), and most importantly our economic-social-and-political system that allow corporations to be concerned with little beyond the bottom line. We only have ourselves to blame for allowing BP's negligence, which, of course, it blames on the company it leased the oil rig from: Transocean. But, again, who expects a multi-billion dollar company to take responsibility for its mess?

We also can't blame President [Barack] Obama for opening up millions of acres to offshore drilling, because this is what politicians do: they compromise. With pressure from Republicans and the oil industry, with a desire to win broader support on a faltering climate and energy bill, and with a chance to show he was all about turning the economy around (no matter the cost), Obama chose to open off-shore drilling pretty much everywhere. It wasn't his fault that less than a month later events would make him wish he could take back his words and maybe even his decision.

We can't blame the mainstream media for not better preparing us for the realities of off-shore drilling—or even for that matter the environmental and human costs of drilling anywhere—because enough viewers continue to consume big media even when it has become sensationalized entertainment rather than informative journalism. Although our media focuses more on ideology than substance, pursues its facts from talking heads over actual experts, and thrives on bombast rather than sense, enough of us still watch to keep subpar, ideological, and often insulting programs on the air.

So, in the end the only ones we can blame are ourselves.

Few Stood up Against More Drilling

Finally, we can't simply sit-back and blame the people chanting 'drill, baby, drill', because who was standing up on the other side? Who was speaking out to keep drilling off of our coastlines, away from our wildlife, our beaches, and our fishing grounds? Who was calling for an end to the fossil fuel era—and instead spending money and resources pursuing clean energy, greater efficiency, and encouraging less consumption? Who was on the other side organizing rallies, pressing legislators, and giving a voice to: 'wind, baby, wind' or 'solar, baby, solar'? Not our leaders, not our media, and not even many of those who actually understood that one can't drill without consequences. I admit that some were there, yes, a few stood tall, but let's be honest, most of us didn't do that much. Maybe sent a few e-mails, made a few calls, but where was the uprising after Exxon Valdez [oil spill in 1989] or Ixtoc 1 [oil spill in 1979] or the Chevron debacle (that continues today) in Ecuador [a lawsuit begun in 1993 in which Ecuador claims Chevron polluted part of the Amazon rainforest]?

So, in the end the only ones we can blame are ourselves, and this is why we get the oil spill we deserve.

A Warning to End Fossil Fuel Use

If any good is to come from any of this, it will come in the form of America finally moving from being fossil fuel-driven to a clean-energy driven. I hope this spill is not for nothing: I hope it forces BP and other energy corporations to start regulating themselves; I hope it convinces President Obama to place a moratorium on offshore drilling and heavily invest in green energy; I hope it convinces the media to take issues more seriously as their reporting—or lack thereof—has real world consequences; and I hope it convinces the 'drill, baby, drill' people that political slogans have power and sometimes a price: so, use wisely.

In the end I hope it forces all of us to take a look at fossil fuel-driven world and to realize it doesn't have to be this way. We have long possessed the technology to move toward an oil and coal-free world, we only need the will.

But I'm not counting on any of these changes to occur. So if, like with Exxon Valdez, another twenty years goes by and once again we have a massive catastrophic spill—this time let's say from one of those new oil wells to be built off the coast of Virginia—we'll have no one to blame but ourselves.

3

Environmentalists Are Partly to Blame for the Oil Spill

Charles Krauthammer

Charles Krauthammer is a Pulitzer Prize-winning columnist, writer, and political analyst whose work has been syndicated in several newspapers, including the Washington Post. *He is a regular contributor to Fox News and often appears as a panelist on the station's television program* Special Report with Bret Baier.

The April 20, 2010 British Petroleum (BP) oil spill has many culprits. BP is certainly responsible for its own equipment and engineering faults, and the government is accountable for continually downplaying the risks and environmental impact of a potential spill. However, one group, the environmentalists, has seemingly escaped blame for their part in this catastrophe. It was environmentalists, after all, who fought to ban oil drilling in Alaska and in shallower waters of the Atlantic and Pacific Oceans where the damage caused by a spill might have been mitigated more easily. By forcing oil companies to drill deep—where capping leaks can be problematic—environmentalists should shoulder some of the responsibility for the disaster.

Here's my question: Why were we drilling in 5,000 feet of water in the first place?

Many reasons, but this one goes unmentioned: Environmental chic has driven us out there. As production from the shallower Gulf of Mexico wells declines, we go deep (1,000 feet and more) and ultra deep (5,000 feet and more), in part because environmentalists have succeeded in rendering the Pacific and nearly all the Atlantic coast off-limits to oil production. (President [Barack] Obama's tentative, selective opening of some Atlantic and offshore Alaska sites is now dead.) And of course, in the safest of all places, on land, we've had a 30-year ban on drilling in the Arctic National Wildlife Refuge.

So we go deep, ultra deep—to such a technological frontier that no precedent exists for the April 20 blowout in the Gulf of Mexico.

One Disaster, Many Culprits

There will always be catastrophic oil spills. You make them as rare as humanly possible, but where would you rather have one: in the Gulf of Mexico, upon which thousands depend for their livelihood, or in the Arctic, where there are practically no people? All spills seriously damage wildlife. That's a given. But why have we pushed the drilling from the barren to the populated, from the remote wilderness to a center of fishing, shipping, tourism and recreation?

The federal government can fight wars, conduct a census and hand out billions in earmarks, but it has not a clue how to cap a one-mile-deep out-of-control oil well.

Not that the environmentalists are the only ones to blame. Not by far. But it is odd that they've escaped any mention at all.

The other culprits are pretty obvious. It starts with BP, which seems not only to have had an amazing string of perfect-storm engineering lapses but no contingencies to deal with a catastrophic system failure.

However, the railing against BP for its performance *since* the accident is harder to understand. I attribute no virtue to

BP, just self-interest. What possible interest can it have to do anything but cap the well as quickly as possible? Every day that oil is spilled means millions more in losses, cleanup and restitution.

Federal officials who rage against BP would like to deflect attention from their own role in this disaster. Interior Secretary Ken Salazar, whose department's laxity in environmental permitting and safety oversight renders it among the many bearing responsibility, expresses outrage at BP's inability to stop the leak, and even threatens to "push them out of the way."

"To replace them with what?" asked the estimable, admirably candid Coast Guard Adm. Thad Allen, the national incident commander. No one has the assets and expertise of BP. The federal government can fight wars, conduct a census and hand out billions in earmarks, but it has not a clue how to cap a one-mile-deep out-of-control oil well.

Obama didn't help much with his finger-pointing Rose Garden speech in which he denounced finger-pointing, then proceeded to blame everyone but himself. Even the grace note of admitting some federal responsibility turned sour when he reflexively added that these problems have been going on "for a decade or more"—translation: [George W.] Bush did it—while, in contrast, his own interior secretary had worked diligently to solve the problem "from the day he took office."

Really? Why hadn't we heard a thing about this? What about the September 2009 letter from Obama's National Oceanic and Atmospheric Administration accusing Interior's Minerals Management Service of understating the "risk and impacts" of a major oil spill? When you get a blowout 15 months into your administration, and your own Interior Department had given BP a "categorical" environmental exemption in April 2009, the buck stops.

Expectations of the President

In the end, speeches will make no difference. If BP can cap the well in time to prevent an absolute calamity in the gulf, the president will escape politically. If it doesn't—if the gusher isn't stopped before the relief wells are completed in August—it will become Obama's Katrina [the hurricane that struck the Gulf Coast in 2005].

That will be unfair, because Obama is no more responsible for the damage caused by this than Bush was for the damage caused by Katrina. But that's the nature of American politics and its presidential cult of personality: We expect our presidents to play Superman. Helplessness, however undeniable, is no defense.

Moreover, Obama has never been overly modest about his own powers. Two years ago next week [in 2008], he declared that history will mark his ascent to the presidency as the moment when "our planet began to heal" and "the rise of the oceans began to slow."

Well, when you anoint yourself King Canute [Norwegian King and Viking commander associated with a legendary ability to control the tides], you mustn't be surprised when your subjects expect you to command the tides.

4

The George W. Bush Administration Is to Blame for the Oil Spill

Matthew Yglesias

Matthew Yglesias is a fellow at the Center for American Progress Action Fund, a progressive think tank. He contributes to political news websites and is the author of Heads in the Sand: How the Republicans Screw Up Foreign Policy and Foreign Policy Screws Up the Democrats.

While the Gulf of Mexico oil disaster occurred during the presidency of Barack Obama, the roots of the problem lay in policies enacted under the George W. Bush administration. The Bush-era government favored rampant oil drilling and disregarded environmental protections in order to satisfy industry interests. Federal agencies, staffed by pro-business cronies, ignored scientists' warnings about the potential hazards of a deep-water oil spill in order to keep oil profits flowing. Such indifference to the consequences of drilling was a hallmark of the Bush administration, and the Obama administration is still trying to recover from these policies.

Ever since the great oil price spike of 2008, conservatives have been riding a tide of pro-drilling sentiment to shore up their message on energy issues. Environmentalists had done a decent job in earlier years of framing their concerns about fossil-fuel use in part in terms of energy "independence" and "security," rhetoric that was turned on its head by efforts like [former Speaker of the House] Newt Gingrich's "Drill Here, Drill Now, Pay Less" slogan. The push was so successful that the [Barack] Obama administration somewhat reluctantly came around to the pro-drilling viewpoint just in time for the largest oil spill in human history to hit the Gulf of Mexico—pushing public support for drilling down for the first time in years. This left the hard-core drillers of the right like Gingrich and Karl Rove [Deputy Chief of Staff to President George W. Bush] to grasp for the argument that the spill is somehow "Obama's Katrina"—a charge so absurd that even Fox News hosts won't buy it. Meanwhile, new revelations in Friday's [May 14, 2010] *New York Times* reveal that something closer to the reverse is the truth—the Deepwater Horizon fiasco is yet another consequence of George W. Bush's corruption and incompetence.

The dysfunctional attitude of MMS [Minerals Management Service] managers reflected problems that were deeply ingrained under the previous administration.

A Bush-Era Agency at the Heart of the Problem

The key to the puzzle is an obscure agency known as the Minerals Management Service [MMS], which manages energy resources on federal land and the outer continental shelf. The mission of the agency is supposed to be to ensure that these resources are used responsibly and that taxpayers get a fair share of the revenue associated with their exploitation. But under the Bush administration, it, like so many agencies, was turned into a plaything of industry leading to numerous ecological catastrophes.

The key facts have been in the press, but the political implications and the timeline are still not well understood. For starters, as Juliet Eilperin reported [in the *Washington Post*], back on April 6, 2009, the MMS chose to give the Deepwater Horizon project a "categorical exclusion" from the National Environmental Policy Act's requirement for a detailed examination of possible environmental impacts. What's more, as Ian Urbina reported in the Times Thursday [May 13, 2010], MMS also simply ignored warnings from the National Oceanic and Atmospheric Association [NOAA] and MMS' own scientists that the drilling represented a threat to endangered species. Specifically, a September 2009 letter from NOAA "accused the minerals agency of a pattern of understating the likelihood and potential consequences of a major spill in the Gulf and understating the frequency of spills that have already occurred there." Urbina reported that a half-dozen current or former MMS scientists told him that "managers at the agency have routinely overruled staff scientists whose findings highlight the environmental risks of drilling."

By 2009, of course, Barack Obama was already in the White House. But it takes time to staff an administration and take charge of an agency. Current MMS director Liz Birnbaum didn't take office until July 2009, months after the exclusion was granted. More to the point the dysfunctional attitude of MMS managers reflected problems that were deeply ingrained under the previous administration.

Expanding the Royalties in Kind Program

Consider, for example, the fiasco of the Royalty in Kind program. The saga starts back in 1997 when, under Bill Clinton, the government cared about doing things properly. At this point in time, MMS responded to evidence that energy interests were underpaying royalties to the federal government by proposing a more stringent rule to collect Royalties in Value (RIV), i.e., money from drillers and miners. Industry didn't like that and countered instead with a proposal to pay Royalties in Kind (RIK), i.e., oil or gas that they thought would be cheaper. The Clinton administration agreed to an RIK pilot program, but soon found itself out of office. Then along came the Bush administration and [Vice President] Dick Cheney's Energy Task Force, which was urged by the American Petroleum Institute to aggressively expand the program. Starting in 2003, the Government Accountability Office repeatedly issued criticisms of the RIK program on a nearly annual basis saying it lacked "clear strategic objectives linked to statutory requirements" and shouldn't be expanded.

This, of course, was the very essence of the Bush administration approach to government. When a regulator could be staffed by shills for the industry it was supposed to oversee, it was.

But it was steadily expanded each and every year of the Bush administration because statutory requirements aside, RIK was great at achieving the president's objective of letting oil companies make more money. By September 2009, a new team was in charge and Secretary of the Interior Ken Salazar announced the program would be terminated.

The RIK scam, of course, was not the cause of the oil spill any more than failure to consult NOAA about endangered species implications did the deed. Both incidents, however, reflect the existence of a culture of indifference to the substantive missions of government agencies. This, of course, was the very essence of the Bush administration approach to government. When a regulator could be staffed by shills for the industry it was supposed to oversee, it was. When no industry particularly wanted to own an agency, like FEMA [Federal Emergency Management Agency], it was handed over to a random crony. The results were disastrous [as when FEMA sluggishly responded to Hurricane Katrina in 2005] and we're still paying the price today.

5

The Obama Administration Response to the Oil Spill Is Lacking

Jeff Crouere

Columnist and political analyst Jeff Crouere is the host of Ringside Politics *on WLAE television, a PBS station in New Orleans.*

The presidential administration of Barack Obama is not acting fast enough or with much fervor to contain the disastrous consequences of the Gulf of Mexico oil spill, which has ruined much of the Louisiana coastline. The President should use federal resources—including the military—to stop the spread of oil, and he should mobilize civilian volunteers to assist in the clean-up. Instead Obama has left Louisiana to fend for itself while he flies off on vacations and politicking tours.

The excuses are wearing thin. The tough talk has been exposed as nonsense. At this point, it is clear that British Petroleum (BP) and the [Barack] Obama Administration are making it up as they go along.

Despite bravado from Interior Secretary Ken Salazar about taking over the oil spill effort from BP, Coast Guard Commander Thad Allen dismissed this as just a "metaphor." Allen claims that only BP has the expertise and the equipment to deal with the oil spill. He even says that he trusts BP, making Allen the only person in the world with such confidence in the British polluters.

Trusting BP to Resolve the Problem

It is amazing to think that the federal government has been approving deep-water drilling without any real plan in case of a blowout. So far, every tactic that BP has tried has failed and the prospects for their latest gambit, the "top kill," are uncertain at best. BP has pushed back the start of this newest attempt to stop the oil spill several times.

In the meantime, the Obama Administration seems to be content to trust BP to lead the effort, but the disgusted people of South Louisiana want more action. In fact, they are demanding leadership. Obama's strategy is even troubling such highly partisan Democrats as political consultant James Carville. According to Carville, "They're risking everything by this go along with BP strategy." He called the administration's response to the crisis "lackadaisical."

The President Needs to Take Action

In a crisis, leaders emerge and deal effectively with the emergency. In this environmental disaster, Barack Obama has been disengaged, has made very few comments on the situation and has shown a total lack of leadership. He is more interested in pinning blame on BP and creating a federal commission to investigate the accident. There will be plenty of time for investigations, but now is the time to halt the leak, contain the spill and clean up the mess. While the Obama Administration tries to play politics, the Louisiana coast is dying.

The President has not held a real news conference in months, so he has not answered any serious questions about his administration's lame response to this crisis. In the past 35 days, his only feeble attempt to deal with the media consisted of answering two questions from the foreign press about illegal immigration.

The truth is that, from the very beginning, Obama has given this monumental problem only scant attention. Is Obama moving so tentatively because of his close ties to BP?

According to the Center for Responsive Politics, Obama was the largest recipient of campaign contributions from BP in the last election cycle, receiving $77,051.

Is it because the spill is happening off the coast of a red state? There seems to be little doubt that if this tragedy occurred off the coast of California or New York, there would be more urgency from the White House. Former Alaska Gov. Sarah Palin said that President Obama has been taking too "doggone long to get in there, to dive in there and grasp the complexity and the potential tragedy that we are seeing here."

Sadly, the President is placing politics over this disaster and reinforcing the suspicion shared by many in Louisiana that he does not care about this issue or the damage being done to the wetlands.

As the invasion of oil continues and the marsh dies, desperate Louisiana officials are trying to move forward with a plan to build a series of barrier islands to capture the oil. Yet, the dredging project cannot begin because the necessary permits have not been issued by the U.S. Army Corps of Engineers.

After five weeks of inaction, no local or state official should have to ask for any more approval from federal agencies. No one should wait another minute for help that may never arrive. Louisiana Gov. Bobby Jindal complained that he was "frustrated" by the slow governmental response. Plaquemines Parish President Billy Nungesser is also disgusted by the lack of leadership and action from both BP and the federal government. He is so upset that at the next council meeting he will request emergency funding so the parish can begin the barrier project immediately. The parish has access to the equipment and the personnel to complete the project, which should be billed to British Petroleum.

Politics Over Disaster Relief

On the federal level, the President should convene a meeting of the top leaders in the oil and gas industry to develop an action plan. He should direct the military to offer whatever assistance is necessary to stop the oil volcano from gushing into the gulf and to clean up the disaster in the marsh. The National Guard should be mobilized to the region and recreational boaters and fisherman should be utilized to tow containment booms and skim the oil from the surface. Volunteers should be recruited from around the Gulf Coast to hit the beaches to clean up the remains of the oil.

Instead of creating an aggressive action plan to deal with the crisis, the President is spending today traveling to California to campaign for U.S. Senator Barbara Boxer. Sadly, the President is placing politics over this disaster and reinforcing the suspicion shared by many in Louisiana that he does not care about this issue or the damage being done to the wetlands. To make matters even worse, the President is getting ready to take his second vacation since this crisis started and has played golf several times since the oil spill occurred. If a Republican President were responding to this disaster in such a cavalier manner there would be a media firestorm. In this case, the media has given the President a pass and focused their attention on British Petroleum, but, in reality, both deserve criticism.

It is time for the people of Louisiana to take matters into their own hands. The excuses, inaction and finger-pointing from the twins of incompetence—British Petroleum and the Obama Administration—are pathetic and are just making this horrific disaster even worse. This catastrophe reminds us once again that the best way for local communities to deal with a crisis is to respond aggressively and not wait for official approval. Remember, it is easier to ask for forgiveness than it is to get permission.

6

The Environmental Damage from the Oil Spill Has Been Downplayed

Orpheus Reed

Orpheus Reed is a columnist for Revolution, *voice of the Revolutionary Communist Party, USA.*

The British Petroleum (BP) oil spill in the Gulf of Mexico may be over, but the ecological damage is far from contained. The government and the oil industry want Americans to believe the threat and harm have passed, but the environmental impact of the oil and oil dispersants has yet to be calculated. As previous oil spills have shown, the harmful effects of these chemicals take their toll over years, not months. So far, researchers have found dead wildlife in the Gulf region, and clean-up workers and shrimpers have reported illnesses thought to be related to the contamination. Much of this has gone unreported by the government because the nation still depends on the profits and energy of the oil industry.

The Gulf of Mexico oil disaster is now officially the largest marine oil spill in world history. The damage that has been done is incalculable, and damage is still going on. But the government, which has lied about this crisis all along, is trying to tell people, "Move along, it's all over here."

A huge pool of oil and dispersants has covered large swaths of the Gulf, most under the water's surface. For more than

100 days, this toxic mess has been the environment in which thousands of marine species have had to try to survive. Six hundred miles of Gulf coastline have been hit, the grasses that hold the wetlands together have been bathed in oil and oil has been buried in sediments (materials found at the bottom of a body of water). Oil has spread across estuaries—the nurseries of life in the Gulf. Thousands of people have been poisoned, children sickened with burning eyes, rashes, nausea, and headaches.

BP, the government, and the mainstream media are saying that BP's cap on the well will hold and that the oil gusher may finally be stopped. Should we believe them? All of them have consistently lied about, minimized, and covered up this catastrophe at every stage. They have prevented independent observers from access to data and prevented independent investigations to verifying BP claims. But even if the well turns out to be finally capped, what has already unfolded is the largest environmental catastrophe in U.S. history. Waters rich with life are now polluted by at least 172 million gallons of oil and 1.8 million gallons of chemical dispersants.

Has the Disaster Been Averted?

Yet now, we are told by the federal government and the mainstream media that magically this immense toxic mass of oil has largely disappeared, and what's left poses little ongoing threat. That case is made in an August 4 [2010] report from the National Oceanic and Atmospheric Association (NOAA). A *New York Times* headline read, "U.S. Finds Most Oil From Spill Poses Little Additional Risk."

White House spokesperson Robert Gibbs claimed, "I think it's fairly safe to say that because of the environmental effects of Mother Nature, the warm waters of the Gulf and the federal response, that many of the doomsday scenarios that were talked about and repeated a lot have not and will not come to fruition."

BP has already scaled back clean-up efforts, even as on August 1 Louisiana authorities cited dozens of reports of oil as sheen, tar balls, and thick goo spread across five parishes (counties) in the Mississippi Delta region.

The truth is that the gush of oil may be stopped, but this catastrophe is far from over. The line that there is little threat is an outrageous lie. Disastrous consequences—to people's health, to their livelihood and ability to even continue to live in the places they love, to the beautiful and rich ecosystems of the Gulf—are only beginning to be felt and will continue for years to come.

People must insist that the full scope of the damage be uncovered.

Those claiming we can now "put all this behind us" are representatives of the same government and the same capitalist system that allowed BP to drill 5,000 feet deep in the ocean without any plan for how to stop a gusher like this at this depth. They signed off on drilling without environmental review. They are the same ones that lied about the amount of oil pouring out. They attacked scientists who revealed huge plumes of oil in the Gulf. They speak for a government, and a whole system, that failed to respond in the way needed to this catastrophe.

Now they want everyone to "just move on" from a catastrophe which revealed the capitalist system's utter inability to protect the people and the ecosystems. Now they are attempting to walk away and cover up their crime. People must insist that the full scope of the damage be uncovered. This must be fought for, and people must demand that the needs of people in the Gulf and the ecosystems be met, that this disaster be addressed and stopped.

Deep Oceans Poisoned by Dispersed Oil

NOAA's report says 74% of the oil that poured from the gusher has been captured, burned, dispersed, evaporated, or "dissolved," and 26% is left in the Gulf.

Even if NOAA's figures were to be accepted, over 100 million gallons (of a total of 206 million) remains in the Gulf in one form or another. This is no case for "the threat is behind us." About half of this 100 million gallons is oil dispersed in the water, which NOAA claims is essentially no threat. This is untrue. A body of scientific evidence shows chemically dispersed oil is actually more toxic than oil alone. And the toxic components of "naturally dispersed oil" are still present, just mixed into the water.

Scientist Samantha Joye, who first reported the underwater plumes of oil, has said that "the fact that this oil is 'invisible' makes it no less of a danger to the Gulf's fragile ecosystems. Quite the contrary, the danger is real and . . . is much more difficult to quantify, track, and assess."

Many scientists have criticized the report for shaky methodology. Others said it was just putting a spin on things to make the Gulf and federal clean-up look as good as possible.

NOAA's report is being used to say there is little remaining threat, but the report says nothing about the effect of all this oil over months and months on all the life present in the Gulf! In fact, no government agency has yet to really study this. What is known is that this mix of oil with dispersants is very toxic, especially to the larvae and young life forms present in Gulf waters this spring and summer. This is an indictment of the total failure by this government, which concentrates the power of this capitalist system, to safeguard the environment.

BP and the government sprayed unprecedented amounts of Corexit dispersants to break up the oil on the surface and at the wellhead. Claiming dispersants were "less toxic than oil," they used the chemical to push the oil under the surface where the political cost of contamination would be less than oil hitting large portions of the coastline. What the federal Environmental Protection Agency (EPA) called a "trade-off" has meant sacrificing marine life.

A Scientist Consensus Statement on dispersants shows that Corexit dispersants mixed with oil "pose grave health risks to marine life and human health, and threaten critical niches in the Gulf food web that may never recover." Dispersants allow the toxic compounds of oil to pass more easily into the cells and tissues of organisms. Dispersed oil can damage "every system in the body," according to the statement. Human health effects include burning skin, difficulty breathing, headaches, heart palpitations, dizziness, confusion, and nausea. Chemically dispersed oil can cause serious and long-term impacts— lung, liver, and kidney damage; immune system suppression; and neurological damage in children and developing fetuses.

The EPA, the government agency charged with protecting health, has instead assisted BP in poisoning the Gulf and its people.

Even some scientists within EPA raised questions to supervisors about dispersants, but their concerns were disregarded. Despite saying BP should restrict dispersant use to "rare cases" a Congressional committee revealed that the Coast Guard approved requests from BP to spray dispersants 74 times in 54 days.

Another danger present in the Gulf is the potential for creating larger areas of dead zones, areas where marine life is killed off from lack of oxygen in the water. Joye's team, and other scientific teams, discovered oxygen levels within the oil plumes were 30–50% below normal. Microbes in the water feed on oil and methane gas (which also poured from the well), and use up oxygen as they feed on the oil. If oxygen drops too far, dead zones can be created. Dead zones already appear every summer in the Gulf and the oil disaster could make this worse.

Ongoing Damage to Food Webs and Human Health

Gulf food webs face real danger. Thousands of animals have been found dead—likely only a portion of those that died. Die-offs of fish and pyrosomes—a food organism that endangered sea turtles and others feed on—have been discovered. Scientists have found that droplets of oil have been incorporated into the shells of young crabs, a food mainstay for many organisms.

The 1989 *Exxon Valdez* spill in Alaska, which poured 16 times *less*, oil into the water than the Gulf spill, caused severe long-term damage to the ecosystems, much of which showed up years later. The spill had multi-leveled impacts. Toxic components entered the food web. Species like sea ducks and marine mammals suffered high mortality for years because they ate creatures contaminated by hidden oil and brought up buried oil when they dug for prey.

Many workers on the spill have gotten sick.

The government claim that similar or worse impacts won't happen in the Gulf is a cover-up. The Gulf catastrophe has devastated people's livelihoods—thousands of fishermen out of work, businesses shut down. Many fishermen involved in cleaning the oil face being thrown out of work again as BP scales back the clean-up. Whole communities of many diverse cultures have lived in the bayous of south Louisiana for generations or more. Now many are confronting whether they will be forced to leave, even if their communities will continue to exist, because the rich life in the marshes they depend on is being poisoned.

Many workers on the spill have gotten sick. Susan Shaw, a toxicologist with the Marine Environmental Research Institute, told CNN that shrimpers exposed to dispersed oil have reported heart palpitations, muscle spasms, and rectal bleeding. In a survey of 1,200 Gulf residents living near the coastline by a public health group from Columbia University, more than one-third said their children had problems with rashes and breathing, or are more nervous, fearful, or sad since the catastrophe.

Economic Concerns Still Trump Environmental Concerns

Oil is an essential factor in the global capitalist economy, and control over that oil is critical to the dominant position of the U.S. empire. *That*—not the needs of humanity or the planet—has framed everything about this system's response to the Gulf oil catastrophe. Limited studies are done that blandly report results without any conclusions as to what real threats are or in a way that people can understand them. They downplay impacts on ecosystems and human health. They spin numbers to make things look good. Many things are simply not studied at all. The logic here is not to get at the truth, but to cover it up, and to get back to business as usual. Again, capitalist logic: the logic of the "bottom line."

This capitalist system has turned the Gulf into a laboratory filled with thousands of oil rigs. This is the Gulf's fundamental "worth" and "meaning" to this system. The environment is seen as simply a means to an end, its resources to be plundered and poured into production for profit. There is no long-term planning about the future dangers to the ecosystems. Everything is sacrificed to the need to get back to business as usual, especially to drilling for oil—which is a lifeblood of this system. This is, indeed, a system utterly unfit to be the planet's caretaker.

Now the skids are being greased to quickly overturn [Barack] Obama's short-term and partial moratorium on deep water drilling and to "drill baby drill." Obama's "truth" commission is not even expected to wait until the moratorium ends in November to allow drilling to resume. Obama has made clear offshore drilling remains central to U.S. energy policy. Obama claims "the best science and the needs of people of the Gulf" is guiding the government response, but this is a hollow lie.

This is a huge crime in active motion. It must be opposed and resisted. Studies need to be done, people's health monitored and protected, people's livelihoods and communities need to be saved, and the damage to ecosystems addressed.

7

The Environmental Damage from the Oil Spill Has Been Exaggerated

Lou Dolinar

Lou Dolinar is a retired columnist for Newsday. *He is currently working on a book covering the British Petroleum (BP) oil spill in the Gulf of Mexico.*

Though an unfortunate accident, the BP oil spill in April 2010 has not produced the dire consequences many environmentalists and news agencies predicted. The oil has not spread very far, and most has been dissolved harmlessly into the gulf waters. The regional ecosystems will be able to tolerate the miniscule amounts of oil found in the water just as they have always been able to safely absorb natural oil leaks from the gulf floor. Even the alarms about the toxicity of dispersants used to contain the oil spill are unjustified, leading some to rightly fret over the economic damage to the oil industry and tourist trade that such unnecessary panic and bogus speculation will cause.

Four months after the *Deepwater Horizon* spill [in April 2010]—which President [Barack] Obama called the "worst environmental disaster America has ever faced"—the oil is disappearing, and fisheries are returning to normal. It turns out that this incident exposed some things that are seriously wrong in the world of oil—and I don't mean exploding wells. There was a broad-based failure on the part of the media, the

Lou Dolinar, "Our Real Gulf Disaster," *National Review*, August 30, 2010, pp. 30–32. NationalReview.com. © National Review Online 2010. All Rights Reserved. Reproduced by permission.

science establishment, and the federal bureaucracy. With the nation and its leaders looking for facts, we got instead a massive plume of apocalyptic mythology and threats of Armageddon. In the Gulf, this misinformation has cost jobs, lowered property values, and devastated tourism, and its effects on national policy could be deep and far-reaching.

News reports implied or asserted that 'enormous oil plumes' were waiting, like submerged monsters, to rise and attack unsuspecting beaches and wetlands.

Faulty Models and Erroneous Speculation

To get an idea of the scale of misinformation involved, consider how many of the most widely reported narratives about the spill—phones that have woven their way into the national consciousness—have turned out to be dubious. Some examples:

East Coast beaches are threatened. Everyone got the wrong idea about the magnitude of the spill from the very beginning. Simply put, while terrible, it was never going to be as big as most thought it would be. The spreading of this East Coast-beach meme was a joint operation of NCAR, the National Center for Atmospheric Research, and the media. In June, NCAR produced a slick computer-modeled animated video that showed a gigantic part of the spill making its way around the southern tip of Florida and up the East Coast. Oil covered everything from the Gulf to the Grand Banks. "BP oil slick could hit East Coast in weeks: government scientists," dutifully reported the New York *Daily News*. CBS News, MSNBC, and many other media outlets chimed in in the same vein. The video was wildly popular on YouTube.

But then the government, in the form of a more senior bureaucracy, the National Oceanographic and Atmospheric Administration (NOAA), disavowed the scenario.

In fact, according to Chuck Watson of Watson Technical Consulting—a Savannah, Ga., firm specializing in computer modeling of the effects of hurricanes, seismic events, geophysical hazards, and weapons of mass destruction—the simulation was bogus from the very beginning, because it ignored important conditions in the Gulf. Furthermore, says Watson, the media never took account of how diluted the oil would be once it hit the Atlantic: The bulk of the theoretically massive spill the video shows amounts to roughly a quart of oil per square mile. Watson claims flat-out that NOAA was "gold digging" for grants; there's probably more federal research money floating around the Gulf than there is oil. "There is a feeding frenzy with people trying to get funding for their specialty," he says.

Giant plumes of oil. By mid-May, oil was still comparatively scarce in the Gulf. Disappointed, the media began trying to figure out where it had gone. Marine researchers were drafted to provide the answer. Diluted oil was being found beneath the surface; but how diluted, no one was sure, and there was nothing vaguely resembling peer-reviewed literature.

Still, news reports implied or asserted that "enormous oil plumes" were waiting, like submerged monsters, to rise and attack unsuspecting beaches and wetlands. The *New York Times* summed up the media consensus on May 15: "Scientists are finding enormous oil plumes in the deep waters of the Gulf of Mexico, including one as large as 10 miles long, 3 miles wide, and 300 feet thick in spots. The discovery is fresh evidence that the leak from the broken undersea well could be substantially worse than estimates that the government and BP have given." The article quoted Samantha Joye, a marine-sciences professor at the University of Georgia, as saying that this oil was mixed with water in the consistency of "thin salad dressing."

According to the *Washington Post*, James H. Cowan Jr., a professor at Louisiana State University, reported "a plume of oil in a section of the Gulf 75 miles northwest of the source of the leak. Cowan said that his crew sent a remotely controlled submarine into the water, and found it full of oily globules, from the size of a thumbnail to the size of a golf ball." The *Post* said that this showed the oil might slip past containment booms and pollute beaches and marshland.

Industry experts say the giant-plume threat was greatly overstated by scientists and further blown out of proportion by the media.

But late in May, NOAA did a study that was far less alarming. It found weak concentrations of oil in the area surrounding the *Deepwater Horizon* site: 0.5 parts per million, maximum. The median was a little over 0.2 parts per million. As with the "giant" spill that threatened the East Coast, that's barely above the threshold of detection. And by late July and early August, BP, the federal government, and some independent researchers were saying they couldn't find any plumes at all. "We're finding hydrocarbons around the well, but as we move away from the well, they move to almost background traces in the water column," said Adm. Thad Allen, the administration's point man on the spill. Some 75 percent of the oil released is gone—and that's based on new estimates that put the spill rate at the high end of earlier projections.

Bogus Threats and Fabricated Fears

As with the bogus doomsday model, industry experts say the giant-plume threat was greatly overstated by scientists and further blown out of proportion by the media. According to Arthur Berman, a respected petroleum expert at Labyrinth Consulting Services in Sugar Land, Texas, the theory flunks basic physics. "Oil is lighter than water and rises above it in all known situations on this planet. The idea of underwater plumes defies everything that we know about physical laws and has distressed me from the outset about these unscientific reports."

It also ignores the Gulf's well-known ability to break down oil. Berman points out that the Gulf has for millennia been a warm, rich ecological gumbo of natural oil seeps, oil-eating bacteria, and marine life that subsists on the bacteria. His research, he says, suggests that the spill represents at most four times as much oil as seeps into the Gulf naturally in a year—in other words, it is eminently digestible by the native ecosystem.

Berman and Watson are contributors to The Oil Drum, a group blog written by and for people in the energy business. The website has been debunking many of the extreme scenarios surrounding the spill. Most of its contributors are proponents of "peak oil" theories, and thus are skeptical of oil's future and eager to explore alternatives. The oil industry has come to a sorry pass when its skeptics are its most credible defenders.

The Corexit threat. No aspect of the spill response has been more controversial than the widespread use of Corexit, a family of detergent-like compounds that break up oil, hence the name "dispersant." Once broken up, oil evaporates, and is also easily eaten by bacteria. Dispersion turns thick, ugly slicks into widely distributed droplets, minimizing damage to beaches and sensitive wetlands. Massive application of dispersants is the reason the spill disappeared so quickly; but it's important not to spray the dispersants directly on living things, like marshlands or coral.

Corexit has faced a variety of criticisms. Some say it is absolutely toxic, even more so when mixed with oil, and blame it for illness, including cancer, among spill workers in Alaska and elsewhere. They claim it's been banned in Britain because it's poisonous. They also suggest that Corexit is more dangerous and less effective than alternative dispersants, and has been used because BP has a financial interest in the firm that makes it. While this full-blown Corexit fear has been the province, for the most part, of green blogs, a few such allegations have made their way into mainstream publications like the *New York Times*, as well as recent congressional hearings.

The reality is that enough of anything will kill you, but that the amount of Corexit in the Gulf is highly diluted. As for the British ban on Corexit, it was based not on toxicity, but on the product's slipperiness: Because the island nation is surrounded by a rocky, ecologically sensitive coastal environment, its version of the EPA [Environmental Protection Agency] makes sure all the small creatures that live there can cling safely to their rocks. If oil or Corexit gets on a rock, the humble limpet, the official guinea pig, loses its grip, so Corexit failed the tests. It is approved for application to spills in open water.

Even the EPA, which tries to ban basically everything but prune juice, has always approved of Corexit under tight supervision. The EPA weighed in with new findings at the beginning of August: It said that Corexit was "similar" in toxicity to other dispersants, and that there was no evil synergistic effect when Corexit was combined with oil. To the extent we need to worry about subtle, long-term environmental problems, the issue of residual oil is 100 times more important than Corexit.

> *Even if the administration quickly rescinds its ban on offshore drilling . . . , the economic impact of the spill and the paranoia surrounding it will be huge.*

Senior scientist Judith McDowell of the Woods Hole Oceanographic Institution, a marine biologist who recently returned from the Gulf, says she isn't entirely comfortable with the compound. But "given the situation in the Gulf," she says, "given the massive amounts of oil and the human-health consequences at the well site, they had no choice." She adds that dispersants should not be used with all spills. "It's a trade-off when one wants to protect shoreline habitats, but you shouldn't apply dispersants in all situations."

The Real Damage of Scaremongering

All this misinformation comes at a serious cost. Even if the administration quickly rescinds its ban on offshore drilling (cost: 50,000 jobs, more than $2 billion in lost wages), as appeared likely in early August, the economic impact of the spill and the paranoia surrounding it will be huge. Potential visitors and customers are scared.

- The real-estate company CoreLogic, as quoted by Bloomberg, says property values could fall by about $3 billion over the next few years along the Gulf, and as much as $56,000 for some houses.

- A trade group, the U.S. Travel Association, said the tourism industry in Florida alone could stand to lose up to $ 18.6 billion over the next three years from the BP oil spill, even though the well has been capped.

- There are dozens of anecdotal reports that no one is buying Gulf seafood, even in areas unaffected by the spill. Gulf Coast shrimpers and fishermen are in a tough spot: On one hand, as more areas of the Gulf are declared safe, they presumably won't be able to collect compensation from BP or the government and will have to get back to work; on the other, no one's buying their catch. Given the public fear of toxins in food, this problem could last a long time.

- Even if the drilling ban ends, regulatory uncertainty will exact a huge cost from oil firms and their shareholders. Some insider reports suggest that oil assets in the Gulf are already being disposed of at fire-sale prices.

What's especially unfortunate here is that all the misinformation connected to overreaction to the spill may have had a serious influence on President Obama and his advisers—leading, for example, to the Gulf drilling ban and an overly strict regulatory approach. This is a tough sell for conservatives, many of whom are looking for evil purposefulness, rather than delusion, in the administration's policies. But think of it this way. We have the most liberal administration in history, and it is composed of people who lack the reflexive skepticism that conservatives apply to the mainstream media and left-wing blogs. Spend enough time following the reporting and blogging on *Deepwater Horizon*, and you come to realize that the administration's behavior in the crisis likely wasn't based on a cynical master plan; rather, the administration was overwhelmed by sheer panic about the magnitude of the potential disasters, outlined by its most loyal supporters, that it thought it faced.

8

The Oil Spill May Be Affecting the Health of Clean-Up Crews

Elizabeth Grossman

Elizabeth Grossman is the author of Chasing Molecules: Poisonous Products, Human Health, and the Promise of Green Chemistry.

In the months after the April 20, 2010 British Petroleum (BP) oil spill in the Gulf of Mexico, clean-up workers and Gulf residents have complained of various ailments including chest pains, dizziness, and breathing problems. Government health agencies and BP have issued reports stating that the risk of health problems caused by the oil is minimal, but no one seems to have definitive proof that the water quality and air quality are not harmful to those in the area. In addition, some researchers are worried that symptoms of illnesses related to the spill may not appear in the short-term and thus could be more injurious over time. So far, confusion reigns in the matter of potential health effects, leaving clean-up crews and locals unsure of how safe it is to live and work in the region.

After more than 100 days of disaster news stories, countless press conferences, and regular updates on government websites, we still have very little real understanding of the Deepwater Horizon blowout's impacts—short- or long-term—on the ocean ecosystem, Gulf Coast communities, or response workers. Environmental-monitoring data released by federal agencies and BP, while copious, fails to answer the

Elizabeth Grossman, "No Comment," *Earth Island Journal*, vol. 25, no. 3, Autumn 2010.

many questions prompted by reported health complaints. Compounding this dilemma is the fact that information is being actively withheld.

Known Extent of the Spill and Cleanup

Here's a reminder of what we're grappling with: To date, more than 200 million gallons of petroleum have gushed from the ruptured well, oiling 650 miles of shoreline and closing fishing, at one time or another, in 88,522 square miles of the Gulf of Mexico. To reduce the amount of oil making landfall, almost 2 million gallons of chemical dispersants—themselves petroleum products with unknown long-term environmental impacts—have been sprayed onto the surface of the water and applied underwater, an application unprecedented in scope. In addition, Coast Guard and BP contractors have conducted 411 surface burns, incinerating more than 11 million gallons of oil, another unprecedented number. While marine bacteria has decomposed some of the oil, the rest has simply been displaced, spread out into the water column or sent into the air.

It's also important to remember that Gulf Coast communities are in unusually close proximity to the water, especially in bayou country. In southern Louisiana, water is front yard and backyard. Working boats line the omnipresent waterfront. "I'm on the water. The whole neighborhood is water," Paul McIntyre, a fisherman from Buras, just north of Venice, Louisiana, told me when I was there in June [2010]. He had signed up for Deepwater Horizon response work and was still waiting to be called up. But he was worried about the health risks. "I don't want to get too involved with the oil itself. I don't want my kid spending the next twenty years taking care of me."

Government and Business
Try to Allay Fears

Government agencies and BP have been telling fishermen that there's no reason for such worries. The Environmental Protection Agency (EPA) has been monitoring air quality across the Gulf Coast while the Occupational Health and Safety Administration (OSHA) has collected data on the chemical exposure to workers engaged in cleanup on beaches, on boats offshore, and at staging and decontamination sites. BP has also publicly posted information about injury and illness to its workers, and those reports have been reviewed by the National Institute of Occupational Safety and Health (NIOSH). According to BP, in "the vast majority of cases there are no significant exposures to airborne concentrations of benzene, total hydrocarbons, or dispersant chemicals of interest."

Across the Gulf Coast, cleanup workers have continually complained of health problems.

OSHA concurs. "To the extent we've been able to look into all cases and that NIOSH has, the majority have been heat-related," said Deputy Assistant Secretary of Labor of Occupational Safety and Health, Jordan Barab. "That's been the diagnosis and they've been treated by rehydrating people." OSHA's sampling is "representative," Barab explained, meaning that it captures only a snapshot rather than the whole picture. Thus far, he said, "We haven't seen much, if any, chemical exposures at all."

Workers Complaining of Illness

Yet across the Gulf Coast, cleanup workers have continually complained of health problems. Dozens have reported—and been treated for—symptoms that include chest pains, headaches, dizziness, nausea, racing heartbeat, respiratory problems, and skin irritation, including open sores. More than 300 oil-related health complaints have been reported to the Louisiana Department of Health and Hospitals, more than 240 of these from response workers. As the oil well kept gushing, concern about toxic chemical exposure became a kind of background hum to anxious conversations happening throughout the region.

"I feel really funky when we are out there," Dave Willman, captain of a skimming boat that had been pumping oiled water within five miles of the rig site since late April, told me in July. "When I wake up out there, my heart starts fluttering. I get an immediate headache when I come in contact with crude oil."

"Everyone out there is coughing," he continued. "People are spitting stuff up in the morning and you can feel your blood pressure. I'm 35 years old. I'm a healthy guy. But I don't feel myself. I'm light-headed and get dizzy. I'm getting headaches and my eyes burn. I get mood swings and I can't stop scratching. I don't know how much longer this can go on before it has a detrimental effect."

Unfortunately, the gaps in what we need to know are largest when it comes to the issue of long-term effects of chemical exposure.

Willman's symptoms aren't unique. In May, ten oil spill response workers were medevacked to the West Jefferson Medical Center in Marrero, Louisiana after suffering chest pains, dizziness, headaches, and nausea not far from the rig site. Several complained of breathing oil fumes and unpleasant chemical odors. Some believed they'd been sprayed with chemical dispersants. All were treated and released, with initial diagnoses of heat-related illness and exacerbated pre-existing health conditions.

The headaches, dizziness, and skin itching are consistent with oil-vapor and solvent exposure, according to Dr. Rose Goldman, associate professor of environmental health at the Harvard School of Public Health. "But it's a complex system," she said of potential exposures out on the oiled waters of the

Gulf. There are volatile organic compounds coming off the oil. There may be an oil and water mist mixture. If there's burning nearby, workers will be exposed to smoke and particulates. "I can't say which symptoms are associated with which exposure," she explained, "but careful monitoring should be done so we can find out how best to protect these workers."

Worries About the Long-Term Effects of Exposure

In June, I stopped by West Jefferson Medical Center to speak with Dr. James Callaghan, an ER doctor and vice chief of staff for the hospital, who'd treated the response workers rushed there in May. He explained that their symptoms were consistent with chemical and heat exposure, and can be exacerbated by preexisting conditions. "The short-term effects are not that significant," Dr. Callaghan told me. "What I think is more problematic are the long-term effects. We should be taking more precautions. This is not a sprint, but a marathon."

Unfortunately, the gaps in what we need to know are largest when it comes to the issue of long-term effects of chemical exposure. Many of the volatile organic compounds (VOCs) associated with oil and dispersants being used can produce adverse health effects that may take years to manifest. This is true of direct exposure to these chemicals—some of which are carcinogens—and exposure via inhaled particulates or consumption of contaminated food or water. While government agencies have released a large volume of raw data, much of it lacks the details that would provide a real understanding of conditions in Gulf Coast communities. The explanations offered by officials are often confusing or contradictory.

"EPA's air monitoring to date has found that air quality levels for ozone and particulates are normal on the Gulf coastline for this time of year and odor-causing pollutants associated with petroleum products are being found at low levels," explained the agency website on July 25. According to the EPA, the Centers for Disease Control has reviewed this data and concluded that reported levels of some pollutants "may cause temporary eye, nose, or throat irritation, nausea, or headaches, but are not thought to be high enough to cause long-term harm. These effects should go away when levels go down or when a person leaves the area."

Current safety standards for VOCs [volatile organic compounds] vary widely from agency to agency and are often not sufficiently protective.

But there's no background data to compare new numbers to, although EPA Administrator Lisa Jackson has called the Gulf's general air quality "not healthy."

Varying Safety Standards

Meanwhile, a response-worker training manual from the National Institute of Environmental Health and Safety (NIEHS) cautions: "Even if air sampling shows no detectable levels or very low levels of volatile organic compounds, there still may be health effects present." The NIEHS manual also notes that safety standards do not always include the effects of skin contact, which in the case of oil products (including crude oil, dispersants, and "drilling mud") can have serious impacts— dermatitis and, in some cases, conditions that lead to skin cancer.

Also, relying on detectable odor may not be the best way to gauge safe levels of hydrocarbon compounds, explained Amanda Hawes, an attorney and board member of Worksafe, a California-based NGO [non-governmental organization]. For example, toluene and xylene have a detectable odor only at concentrations that already substantially exceed levels considered dangerous. Adding to concern is the fact that current safety standards for VOCs vary widely from agency to agency and—according to the latest science—are often not suffi-ciently protective. When I spoke to him in July, OSHA Deputy Assistant Secretary Barab called the existing personal exposure limits "totally inadequate."

In addition to this kind of confusion, there's the problem of information that is simply missing. In early June, NOAA conducted two low altitude air-sampling flights over the Deep-water Horizon site and found elevated concentrations of ben-zene, toluene, and other oil-related aromatic compounds. It also found large amounts of black carbon associated with the one controlled burn sampled. But no further analysis is yet available. So as of late July, there is no publicly available data about ongoing near-surface air quality close to the blowout site, where the heaviest oil concentrations have been skimmed and burned—conditions that affect scores of response work-ers.

Three months into this disaster, we still don't know what, apart from heat, may be affecting response workers.

BP Holds Back Its Findings

BP has conducted its own offshore sampling for airborne par-ticulates but has not released this information. NIOSH has encouraged BP to release that data, but it's become clear that such findings are being withheld, not for scientific reasons but because of the inevitable lawsuits. "Most of the data being col-lected now is being collected for litigation," Robert Gagosian, president and CEO of the nonprofit Consortium for Ocean Leadership, told the audience at the Aspen Environment Fo-rum, explaining that the major federal scientific response so far has focused on gathering data for the government's case against BP. Thus, "much of the information obtained from re-search and monitoring will be tied up in the courts rather than being made publicly available and scrutinized," he wrote in a *Washington Post* op-ed.

The extent of BP's information lockdown is remarkable. Nearly all of my calls to BP contractors—environmental service companies conducting response-worker training or environmental monitoring, and those hiring cleanup crews—have gone either unanswered or produced only information available online. Several questions put to state agencies were answered with, "If you find out, please let us know."

No Ones Knows What May Be Affecting Clean-Up Workers

Three months into this disaster, we still don't know what, apart from heat, may be affecting response workers, many of whom have been out on the water for weeks at a time. We still don't know if the oil and dispersants are affecting coastal residents' air. We also don't know if chemicals specific to dispersants have contaminated seafood, since there's been no such testing. And now that the well is capped and surface oil is diminishing, many Gulf residents worry that, in a desire to revive business, authorities may issue premature bills of clean health.

"We're concerned about what we think is a premature opening of state waters to fishing," said Zack Carter of the Mobile-based South Bays Community Alliance. "We've heard from our folks in all three states—that will hurt them in the long run," he said of the Gulf Coast fishing communities.

I experienced first-hand the confusion swirling around the disaster when, in June, I visited Louisiana's Grand Isle State Park. The oil on the beach was easy to spot—rust-red, bathmat-sized blobs, ribbons, and tar balls. A line of bright orange boom lay in the sand. Up the beach, workers wearing safety vests and boots rested in the shade of a tent shelter. Others worked the oil blobs with rakes and shovels. Near the tent shelter—as I would see later in Mississippi, Alabama, and Florida—were piles of white garbage bags containing oil debris.

When I asked the workers if they could tell me what they had been doing, all replied:

"No comment."

"I can't talk to you ma'am."

"I want to keep my job."

They pointed me to their supervisor, who was resting under the shade of the pier. He too said, "No comment," as did the supervisor of a crew in the state park parking lot. No one warned me off the beach, but some Coast Guard officers told me not to cross the orange boom toward the water. At one point, away from active cleanup, I stepped over. No one paid any attention.

On the way back into town I passed a hand-painted sign that said, "We want our beach back." Three months in, we're no closer to knowing when that may happen.

9

The Oil Industry Has Been Destroying Louisiana's Environment for Decades

Oliver Houck

Oliver Houck is a professor of law at Tulane University in Louisiana. His interests are in environmental and criminal law. As part of his 2010 curriculum, he gave a series of lectures on the BP oil spill.

The British Petroleum (BP) oil spill in April 2010 is just the most visible example of the damage the oil industry has done to the state of Louisiana. The marriage between the state government, the oil industry, and the communities now tied to its continued operation has ensured that the state will continue to suffer not only from accidents like the spill but also from the laying of pipeline and the dredging of canals to feed the oil interests. BP, which rakes in huge profits, is already pressing its case to avoid paying for the clean-up of the spill, but the state has been paying for the environmental damage for nearly 100 years and will likely continue to do so unless the marriage can be broken and the industry is made to accept responsibility.

The [April 20, 2010] British Petroleum blowout stripped the cover from one of the most cherished myths of Louisiana and other oil-producing states—that oil development and the environment coexist in happy harmony. Yet, as devas-

Oliver Houck, "Oil and Accountability: Who Will Pay to Fix Louisiana?" *Nation*, July 12, 2010, pp. 11–14. Reprinted with permission from the July 12, 2010, issue of The Nation. For subscription information call 1-800-333-8536. Portions of each week's Nation magazine can be accessed at http://www.thenation.com.

tating as the blowout is—and we may never know the full extent—it pales in comparison with the damage the oil and gas industry has done to southern Louisiana, year in and year out, over nearly a century. President [Barack] Obama alluded to this in his June 15 Oval Office address, when he called for a comprehensive effort to restore Louisiana's coast and wetlands. There is a bill to be paid here too, and it is enormous. The question is whether the State of Louisiana and the US Congress will ask oil and gas corporations to pony up their fair share—which puts Louisiana in a delicate position.

Louisiana's Oil History

No state in the union has been more firmly wedded to the oil and gas industry than Louisiana. No more zealous preachers of the clean oil gospel can be found than the state's politicians, who were elected by oil money (at the high end of industry campaign funding) and have defended the industry from regulation (including wetland protections), reduced its royalties with tax breaks and "royalty holidays" (thereby depriving the US Treasury of some $53 billion in revenues from existing offshore leases) and beaten the drums for opening the Atlantic Coast and the Arctic National Wildlife Refuge to oil development. . . because Louisiana's experience showed oil and the environment to be so compatible. State brochures feature pelicans and oil platforms against the setting sun. The largest exhibit in New Orleans's Audubon Aquarium of the Americas contains the base of an oil rig, around which swim contented fish, framed by the logos of Shell, Chevron and BP. We have improved on Eden.

The real story was always otherwise; it was just rarely told. Oil was first found in Louisiana a hundred years ago, and the finds swiftly moved south to the coastal zone. Oil companies appropriated the coastal parishes, most notoriously Plaquemines, ground zero for the BP slick; Texaco's leases in Plaquemines were arranged by the parish district attorney, who conveniently reported only part of the proceeds to the parish police jury and kept the rest (a fact that is emerging only after his death, in a family feud). Local politicians in their pockets, Texaco et al. had one remaining problem: getting men and equipment to the drill sites and laying pipelines to carry off the gold. In the companies' way were some 5 million acres of coastal marsh, one of the most biologically productive zones in North America.

The industry has laced 8,000 miles of canals and pipelines through the Louisiana wetlands, each one eroding laterally over time, less an assault at this point than a cancer.

Oil Industry Canals Tearing Up the Environment

The solution was soon to come: floating dredges, which would dig canals to the wellheads and more canals for the pipelines. These dredges have worked nonstop ever since. They have ripped through the wetlands of southern Louisiana like bulldozers, severing bayous, drowning adjacent marshes, draining others and introducing salt water from the Gulf of Mexico that sears the plant roots, at which point they disintegrate and the coastal marsh system, made up of billions of stems and roots of living things, falls apart like wet cardboard. There were alternative means of access, but industry rejected them. It could also have backfilled the canals when the job was done, but this too was rejected. The reasons were remarkably like BP's: those approaches would take time, cost money.

The dredging was not occasional, or here or there. It was pandemic. The industry has laced 8,000 miles of canals and pipelines through the Louisiana wetlands, each one eroding laterally over time, less an assault at this point than a cancer. They are supported by larger navigation canals, requested by the industry and built by the ever-willing Army Corps of Engineers. One such canal, the Mississippi River Gulf Outlet, after killing off 39,000 acres of forest and wetlands between New Orleans and the gulf, ushered Hurricane Katrina right into the city [in 2009]. If you drive down any bayou road in southern Louisiana, you will see marsh grasses out the window. If you fly over them in a plane and look down, you see something that looks like northern New Jersey: water roads and open water through isolated patches of green. The next time you fly over, there will be even less green. We have been losing twenty-five square miles of coastal Louisiana every year, in major part to these canals, to serve the oil and gas industry, which has made tidy sums in the bargain. When I last looked, six oil and energy corporations were listed in the world's top ten.

Coast Guard records show 40 million gallons spilled in Louisiana waters over the past ten years from routine oil activity.

An Ongoing Destruction of the Coast

With this understanding, we may return for the moment to the BP disaster. It is bad, particularly for local communities, and the long term is anyone's guess. We still do not know the full *Exxon Valdez* story, and that was in a more confined space, twenty-one years ago. Current estimates of the BP blowout dwarf the *Valdez* spill, which came in at 11 million gallons. Industry-wide, the figures are no more encouraging. Coast Guard records show 40 million gallons spilled in Louisiana waters over the past ten years from routine oil activity. Which amounts to a *Valdez*-class spill every three years. This news, like the canals, went unreported.

Now we have BP on the front pages and reported daily, as it should be. But the sad fact is that the ongoing destruction of the Louisiana coastal zone—by canal, by pipeline, by boat wakes, by the extraction of billions of gallons of subsurface oil, gas and brines—has done far more indelible damage, not only to the landscape but to a way of life that could be sustainable for generations beyond the future of oil down here. Well before the blowout, the oil industry had eaten a lion's share of the coast through processes few were aware of and nobody talked about. Plaquemines Parish has a legitimate beef with BP today as the oil globs come ashore. But the reason nearly half of Plaquemines has disappeared over the past fifty years is that the oil industry, writ large, destroyed it. No one said a word.

It is clear at this point that BP will pay for its blowout and all consequential damages only to the extent they can be proved.

It was all part of the marriage. Required by federal law to operate a coastal zone permitting program, Louisiana issued oil and gas permits like orders at McDonald's: how many would you like today? State employees referred to the industry as their "clients"; members of the general public, and environmentalists in particular, were called "others." (Of course, behind closed doors the names were more graphic.) Their marching orders, like those of the Minerals Management Service later, were to keep the jubilee on track. In the early 1980s I did a study of Louisiana permits over a three-year period; several thousand issued, four denied—none for oil drilling. A New Orleans *Times-Picayune* reporter did an update covering the past five years and found 4,500 permits issued, none denied. Not even the precipitous collapse of the coastal zone—which had, belatedly, caught public attention—could change the attitude or the practice. Saving the coast is one thing, but requiring the oil industry to help save it is beyond local imagination. Louisiana, the state most vulnerable to climate change and sea level rise, leads the charge against EPA [Environmental Protection Agency] regulation of carbon dioxide (letters of opposition from no fewer than four state agencies and the governor, which must be a record) and the president's climate change bill.

Louisiana's Citizens Are Complicit in the State's Destruction

The BP blowout has put Louisiana politics in a bind. "Drill, baby, drill" may be what [former Alaska Governor] Sarah Palin says, but it is what we do, more rampantly and with less restraint than any jurisdiction one would want to emulate. The reaction of Louisianans to the BP blowout has been to protect the industry and its longstanding commitment to what has turned out to be a very dirty (40 million gallons spilled per decade, in an uneventful decade), plainly unsustainable (it will run out, which is why, Palin and pundits to the contrary, the business has gone offshore) and deleterious relationship (disappeared wetlands do not reappear when you stop abusing them; at best they can be re-created in part, and at enormous expense). The blowback within Louisiana against President Obama's moratorium on deepwater drilling in the gulf has been ballistic, even from the coastal communities most at risk. They too, work on the rigs. We are all in this marriage together.

It is clear at this point that BP will pay for its blowout and all consequential damages only to the extent they can be proved. (It is doubtful we will ever know the impacts on sea life and the benthic floor, and few will be subject to dispositive proof.) The cap on BP's liability to private parties is likely to be lifted. A BP executive, probably one with direct supervision over the rig closure, may well go to jail. But in a couple of years this chapter will close. The next chapter will center on how coastal communities and the resources they depend on can survive. Who knows; the plumes may yet move east and deal Louisiana a nasty but glancing blow. When BP's bill is finally paid, however, there will be another one left that eclipses it. Federal and state officials are still struggling to come up with a plan to restore the southern Louisiana landscape. The price is rising, but high-end estimates put it near a mind-blowing $140 billion. Which has required Louisiana politicians to take a new tack.

The industry that has profited enormously from Louisiana while damaging it severely is now campaigning to have American taxpayers pick up the tab [for the oil spill].

For the past fifty years, as the findings of scientists were trickling in, documenting the relationship between oil canals and marsh loss (the graphs are linear: as the canals go in, the land disappears), the state simply denied them. Worse, those who reported their findings say they were demoted or canned, their work labeled extreme, inimical to Louisiana. We remained glued to the image of the pelican and oil rig in holy harmony. As the coastal losses became too apparent to ignore, however—roads were disappearing under high tides—it became clear that Louisiana was going to need major amounts of money. The state has been reluctant to tag the oil industry with the bill, however; after all, we are still married.

Trying to Make America Foot the Bill

This, then, is the new pitch. It is hard to say with a straight face, but here goes: "OK, we have let oil and gas run rampant in our state, and it has wrecked our coastal zone, but, America, we did it all for you! Louisiana has sacrificed itself for the good of the nation. You all drive cars, don't you? So you ought to pay for fixing the harm." Of course, the good of the country was nowhere on Louisiana's radar; the state was pocketing revenue, and that was sufficient reason to kill the zone. The new pitch also affronts a principle of fairness in America that applies equally to giant corporations and the neighbor who borrows your lawn mower: you break it, you fix it. We do not ask taxpayers to repair coal extractor Massey Energy's damage to Appalachia or to abate emissions from chemical plants because we turn on the lights or buy Clorox. These damages belong in the cost of these products, and it is about time they got in there before the environment tanks because taking it is free.

These considerations have not deterred an unlikely coalition of industry and (a few) environmental groups from banding together in something called America's Wetland to help sell the pitch to Congress. The America's Wetland Foundation is funded by Louisiana industries associated with the oil business, overwhelmingly Shell. In short, the industry that has profited enormously from Louisiana while damaging it severely is now campaigning to have American taxpayers pick up the tab. The industry has spawned another initiative to assist, called America's Energy Coast. I do not think I need to describe its theme. The vehicle du jour is a Louisiana bill in Congress that diverts more public offshore royalties to the state. Louisiana gets more of the pie; the rest of America gets less. The oil and gas industry is, of course, fine with the proposal. It pays not a penny more for nearly a century of damage that has left the coast in shreds.

There is a better approach. We have three major actors here, each responsible for a catastrophic loss: the Army Corps of Engineers, which built the major levees and canals; the oil and gas industry, which, for private profit, laid down an even more extensive and damaging web; and the State of Louisiana, which promoted the first two to the hilt, silenced the critics and took its cut. Each, including industry, can now pay its share. We require the chemical industry to clean up old waste sites under Superfund; we ask the same of the coal industry under the Surface Mine Restoration Act. Billing the oil and gas industry for its damages would be nothing new. Then again, this is Louisiana, and we and oil remain faithfully married—at least until the industry leaves us, as it surely will after a few more heady years, with only the memories and a wasted skin.

10

The Oil Industry Supports Many Louisiana and Gulf Region Economies

Joseph R. Mason

A financial economist, Joseph R. Mason is the Chair of Banking at the Ourso School of Business at Louisiana State University and a Senior Fellow at the Wharton School of Business at the University of Pennsylvania.

In response to the April 2010 British Petroleum (BP) oil spill in the Gulf of Mexico, President Barack Obama imposed a temporary moratorium on future deepwater drilling in the region. Unfortunately, this knee-jerk reaction will have serious economic repercussions on the Gulf community as well as the nation as a whole. The state of Louisiana relies on oil revenues, and many workers earn their paychecks from oil industries. In addition, various local businesses and subsidiary contractors depend on thriving communities fed by oil revenues. The ripples extend beyond the region to affect other industries—such as shipping and health care—that cater to businesses that would be harmed by the moratorium. The economic vibrancy of Louisiana and other Gulf ports is tied to oil profits, and any arbitrary cessation of drilling will have disastrous effects that the presidential administration needs to consider.

Joseph R. Mason, "The Economic Cost of a Moratorium on Offshore Oil and Gas Exploration to the Gulf Region," *Save U.S. Energy Jobs*, July 2010. www.saveusenergyjobs .com. © 2010 American Energy Alliance. Reproduced by permission.

The recent *Deepwater Horizon* oil rig disaster and President [Barack] Obama's subsequent Offshore Deepwater Drilling Moratorium ("moratorium"), originally issued on May 30th, have fanned the flames of the already heated debate over the extent to which drilling for oil and natural gas off U.S. coasts should be permitted. Until recently, the U.S. government has withdrawn leases from areas between 3 and 200 miles off the coasts of 20 states for the extraction of oil and natural gas.

A Hurtful Moratorium

Even prior to the April 20th, 2010 explosion on Transocean's *Deepwater Horizon* rig, which was leased to British Petroleum (BP), policymakers argued that the federal moratoria should be renewed. In an effort to respond to the explosion and subsequent oil spill, President Obama issued a moratorium on exploratory deepwater rigs. The President acknowledged that the moratorium would create problems "for the people who work on [offshore] rigs, but for the sake of their safety, and for the sake of the entire region, [the government needs] to know the facts before [they] allow deepwater drilling to continue." These restrictions, however, are causing significant hardship and economic loss to communities already dealing with a historic recession.

The White House issued the moratorium on May 30th, 2010, stating the need to investigate the causes of the spill and to determine if future spills were possible. The moratorium states:

> The Moratorium Notice to Lessees and Operators (Moratorium NTL) issued today directs oil and gas lessees and operators to cease drilling new deepwater wells, including wellbore sidetrack and bypass activities; prohibits the spudding of any new deepwater wells; and puts oil and gas lessees and operators on notice that, with certain exceptions, MMS [Mineral Management Service] will not consider for

six months drilling permits for deepwater wells and for related activities. For the purposes of the Moratorium NTL, "deepwater" means depths greater than 500 feet. . . . Activities necessary to support existing deepwater production may continue, but operators must obtain approval of those activities from the Department of the Interior.

The moratorium banned deepwater drilling activity, but allowed existing production to continue.

The moratorium would produce broad economic losses within the Gulf region and throughout the nation as a whole.

Critics claim that this policy is unjustified, arbitrary, and capricious given the economic harm it will inflict upon communities dependent upon offshore drilling for jobs and revenue. Accordingly, a federal judge in New Orleans blocked enforcement of the moratorium, writing that "[t]he blanket moratorium, with no parameters, seems to assume that because one rig failed and although no one yet fully knows why, all companies and rigs drilling new wells over 500 feet also universally present an imminent danger," justifying the taking of economic value from private sector jobs and firms. Although the Obama administration has already filed an appeal with a higher court, the judge's decision demonstrates the need to consider how the moratorium on offshore drilling will affect the economies of the Gulf states (Louisiana, Texas, Florida, Alabama, and Mississippi), as well as the nation as a whole. Despite these legitimate concerns, the Obama administration issued a new moratorium on July 12th, 2010—which in fact expands on the original moratorium to include all floating facilities. . . .

My estimates suggest that the moratorium would produce broad economic losses within the Gulf region and throughout the nation as a whole. Given the integrated nature of the U.S.

economy, a negative effect in one industry is likely to be felt throughout the country. A significant halt to oil and natural gas exploration and drilling would not just affect upstream and downstream industries, but could also impact state and local governments, as well as small retail stores, education services, healthcare assistance, and a host of other industries.

The moratorium is not economically viable for the Gulf region and it imposes significant economic harm upon the rest of the U.S.

The effective six-month moratorium on offshore oil and natural gas production will result in the loss of approximately $2.1 billion in output, 8,169 jobs, over $487 million in wages, and nearly $98 million in forfeited state tax revenues in the Gulf states alone. Additionally, although a significant portion of oil and natural gas production is localized in the Gulf, the U.S. is a fully integrated economy, so there is an expectation that the loss will "spill-over" into other states. From this spill-over effect, there could be an additional loss of $0.6 billion in output, 3,877 jobs, and $219 million in potential wages nationwide. Moreover, the federal government stands to lose $219 million in tax revenue. These losses are dramatic in both the context of local economies in which the oil industry operates, and on a national scale. . . .

The Benefits of Offshore Drilling

Unfortunately, the moratorium is not economically viable for the Gulf region and it imposes significant economic harm upon the rest of the U.S. . . .

Offshore oil production benefits federal, state, and local onshore economies. Broadly speaking, there are three "phases" of development that contribute to state economic growth: (1) the initial exploration and development of offshore facilities; (2) the extraction of oil reserves; and (3) the refining of crude oil into finished petroleum products. Businesses that support those phases are prevalent in the sections of the Gulf of Mexico that are currently open to offshore drilling. With regard to the exploration and development stage, the U.S. shipbuilding industry, for example, has a strong presence in the Gulf region and benefits significantly from initial offshore oil exploration efforts. This early phase requires specialized exploration and drilling vessels, floating drilling rigs, and miles and miles of steel pipe, as well as highly—educated and specialized labor to staff the efforts; thus, the jobs and businesses involved in the production of these inputs are supported by offshore drilling.

The economic benefits to coastal and state communities from offshore drilling are substantial.

Along with production, onshore personnel work on the oil extraction phase as well. A recent report prepared for the U.S. Department of Energy indicates that Louisiana's economy is "highly dependent on a wide variety of industries that depend on offshore oil and gas production," and that offshore production supports onshore production in the chemicals, platform fabrication, drilling services, transportation, and gas processing industries. Fleets of helicopters and U.S.-built vessels also supply offshore facilities with a wide range of industrial and consumer goods, from industrial spare parts to groceries.

Workers and Businesses Rely on Oil Money

The economic benefits produced by the refining phase are even more widespread than the effects of the two preceding phases. Although capacity is largely concentrated in California, Illinois, New Jersey, Louisiana, Pennsylvania, Texas, and Washington, additional U.S. refining capacity exists throughout the country. As a result, refinery jobs, wages, and tax revenues are more likely to "spill-over" into other areas of the country, including non-coastal states like Illinois.

The economic benefits to coastal and state communities from offshore drilling are substantial. The Associated Press reports that offshore workers from Louisiana, for example, "frequently earn $50,000 a year or more." One in three jobs in coastal Louisiana "is related to the oil and natural gas industry [and] many of the workers earn between $40,000 and $100,000 a year." Louisiana alone could lose up to 10,000 jobs in only a few months. The state of Louisiana estimates that oil and gas production, primarily from the Gulf, supports $12.7 billion in household earnings, "representing 15.4 percent of total Louisiana household earnings in 2005."

Offshore drilling has helped develop the oil industry around the country by encouraging smaller companies to compete for business with larger players.

The moratorium would put a halt to training new workers and cut jobs for workers already employed within the offshore industry. Additionally, offshore workers that lose their jobs due to the moratorium would receive only a fraction of their wages in unemployment benefits. This will directly affect local businesses, many of which were already weakened by Hurricane Katrina in 2005 and Hurricane Gustav in 2008. Some companies in Louisiana, for example, are already worried that after taking on "heavy debts after Hurricane Katrina [they] may not [be] able to take on additional loans."

In response, President Obama asserted that the Small Business Administration "has stepped in to help businesses by approving loans [and] allowing many to defer existing loan payments." This demonstrates a key understanding by the current administration that small businesses in the Gulf will be hit significantly by the moratorium. Additionally, it is unclear how much the approval and deferment of loans will mitigate the substantial losses taken by small businesses in the Gulf. Indeed, a far simpler solution would be to withdraw the moratorium and allow businesses to operate normally.

Wood Mackenzie Research and Consulting's findings about the impact of a six-month moratorium illustrate the extent to which the offshore industry contributes to local and state economies in the nation. Their research shows that as many as 1,400 workers would be left without jobs, and as many as 46,200 jobs, both on—and offshore, would go idle if the 33 drilling platforms were shut down. The report goes on to say that as many as 120,000 jobs could be lost by 2014. Louisiana would lose 3,000 to 6,000 jobs alone in "the first two to three weeks and potentially more than 20,000 Louisiana jobs within the next twelve to eight months."

In addition to onshore businesses, smaller oil companies that stimulate the economy of the region will be crippled by the moratorium. Offshore drilling has helped develop the oil industry around the country by encouraging smaller companies to compete for business with larger players. The *Wall Street Journal* reports that the oil industry in the Gulf of Mexico was largely developed by relatively small oil and gas companies. In the early 1990s "relatively small players like Kerr-McGee, Ocean Energy and Unocal were acquiring acreage in deep water; their finds helped prove the Gulf's worth to bigger brethren like Chevron, Devon Energy Corp. and Anadarko Petroleum Corp., which later bought these companies at a premium." New generations of companies have started exploratory offshore businesses in the Gulf. Cobalt International Energy, for example, is already experiencing delays in its business because the "U.S. government moratorium on drilling would delay the planned drilling of an exploratory well in the Gulf by six months." . . .

Lost Tax Revenues

Decreased output, fewer jobs, and lost wages translate into lower tax collections and decreases in public revenues. The present analysis applies a broad measure of the total tax revenues (from all sources) that federal, state, and local governments will lose from the moratorium on deepwater drilling. . . . This will translate into reduced investment in the local economy, schools, hospitals, and other necessary public services. Again, even absent current economic conditions, cash-strapped communities benefit significantly from the income that oil and natural gas production brings to the table. Taking away this income source could potentially deny communities access to resources necessary to provide important community projects. . . .

Communities around the Gulf and throughout the country will also suffer negative effects associated with decreased economic activity as a result of a moratorium. Those effects flow from the decrease in high-wage, high-skilled employment. For example, a ban on drilling may induce related industries, such as ship builders, to shut down operations. The loss of employees in these industries, in turn, would decrease community demand for health care, education, and other community services that are available to *all* residents (whether they are employed by the drilling facilities or not). Additionally, the resulting loss of tax revenues could cause a reduction in the availability of these services. The oil and gas industry represents a significant portion of the Gulf states' tax revenue. In 2006, "the oil and gas industry paid more than 14 percent of total state taxes, licenses and fees collected by the state of Louisiana . . . [which represents] a substantial portion of Louisiana's budget." . . .

While employment and wage losses may seem palatable on a national scale, many of the job losses would be concentrated in small coastal towns like Port Fourchon, Louisiana (which is home to substantial resources serving Gulf of Mexico offshore production). Indeed, in some communities the decrease in demand associated with lost jobs tied to offshore drilling moratorium may mean the difference between having a local hospital and school or not.

Coastal cities like Port Fourchon experienced significant growth in the last three decades tied to their central role in offshore oil and gas production. Port Fourchon alone services half of all drilling rigs presently operating in the Gulf of Mexico. Furthermore, current plans call for more than half of all new deep water drilling platforms in the Eastern and Central Gulf of Mexico to use towns like Port Fourchon as their service base. Given the concentration of the deep water Gulf of Mexico operations at coastal communities, it is reasonable that the loss to this community from the moratorium will be substantial. Similar small communities stand to lose significantly as a result of the moratorium.

11

BP Is Covering up the Disastrous Consequences of the Oil Spill

Riki Ott

A former fisherwoman and marine toxicologist, Riki Ott is author of Not One Drop: Betrayal and Courage in the Wake of the Exxon Valdez Oil Spill *and director of Ultimate Civics, a project of Earth Island Institute, an environmental activism organization.*

Americans might easily forget the harmful impact of the British Petroleum (BP) oil spill in the Gulf of Mexico because the company is doing its best to downplay the damage to human health and the environment caused by the accident and its clean-up. The company—in collusion with the US government—is keeping citizens away from the coastal lands affected by the oil spill so that no one can assess the devastation. It is also denying the existence of deepwater oil plumes that are harming sealife, and it is refusing to acknowledge the airborne health hazards faced by clean-up crews working in toxic environments. All Americans should demand that they have a voice in how the spill is rectified so that the oil companies cannot simply sweep the accident away and hope that the nation will soon forget the damage.

On July 15 [2010], BP managed to finally seal its broken Macondo wellhead and stop the oil that had been hemorrhaging into the Gulf of Mexico for 87 days. The very next week, as I was driving up the Florida coast, locals kept pointing out to me where cleanup workers were packing up and pulling out. From Crawfordville through to Carrabelle, and Port St. Joe to Pensacola, the booms were disappearing, the crew tents folded up and removed from beaches.

The well had been capped, after all. The gusher had stopped. Game over. Everyone can go home, right?

Not even close. If all goes according to plan, the relief well should provide a more permanent fix. But that hasn't been the nature of this disaster. Every time BP thought it had the solution, something somehow went wrong. At the time of this writing, at least one oil seep had sprung in the ocean floor near the well as the pressure from the plug found other releases; methane, too, looked to be leaking. And BP was, once again, dodging the government's requests for more monitoring.

The Disaster Did Not End with the Capping of the Well

The capping of the geyser will not, unfortunately, mean the end of the Gulf disaster. Don't forget that it took nearly a month after the blowout for the first oil to make landfall. The oil-and-chemical mix will be coming ashore in the water and on the wind long after the relief well delivers on its promise.

> *Our effort to hold BP accountable for its actions is so complicated because US political leaders have opted to leave the criminals in charge of the crime scene.*

I don't share that fact to be discouraging, but only to remind us all that, if we turn our backs on the Gulf now, we will lose the high stakes game that started on April 20 when the Deepwater Horizon exploded. And I mean us—because every American has a stake in this game. This contest is about far more than dollars for damages; it's about our country's ability to hold big corporate criminals accountable to the public interest and ensure that they follow the laws we enact.

That's going to be tough, especially given our national attention deficit disorder. The media will lose its focus soon and shift its gaze to the next catastrophe. Politicians will be tempted to move on to other agendas. But the environment may not recover for years. And the political and legal effort to hold BP to its promise to "make it right" will take a decade at least—if not two.

Leaving BP in Charge of the Clean-Up

I know this because I am a survivor of the 1989 *Exxon Valdez* oil spill—and the 20 years of litigation that followed. The experience completely changed my life. I started as a marine toxicologist, became a commercial fisherwoman, and ended up a democracy activist. I helped start three nonprofit organizations to deal with the lingering social, economic, and environmental harm that Exxon claims never existed. I wrote two books: one on the biological impact of the spill, the other on the emotional impact of disaster trauma and the process of healing. Then I saw it begin all over again. It's strange—discouraging, really—to witness how seamlessly my work went from the Gulf of Alaska to the Gulf of Mexico.

Our effort to hold BP accountable for its actions is so complicated because US political leaders have opted to leave the criminals in charge of the crime scene. As we saw this spring and summer, BP managed most of the response to its spill, with the federal government playing a kind of auxiliary role. Some countries, like Norway; nationalize the cleanup of oil spills. On a visit to Norway in 1990, the year after the Exxon spill, I was escorted through World War II-era bunkers full of protective booms and absorbent material. National Guardsmen kept a sharp lookout for troubled tankers. One explained to me, "We treat oil spills like a war." It was clear that meant a war against the spill, to protect human health and the environment.

Here in the United States, the spiller-in-charge wages a very different war. It's a war to minimize the spiller's legal liabilities, which means it's a war against the truth, the injured people, and the environment. Each decision the spiller makes is filtered through the lens of accounting rather than accountability. BP's every act is motivated by its desire to reduce its legal and financial liabilities—as was Exxon's after the spill in Alaska. This is not a moral judgment, it's just a point of fact. It's how things work in a system where corporations have one legal reason for being: to make money.

This explains why there are two versions of spill reality: what the spiller says is going on, or the "official" industry-government story, and what is really happening, as told in eye-witness accounts.

I came down to the Gulf on a one-way ticket in early May anticipating the dual reality and committed to highlighting the truth as I found it. I hoped to share experiences from the *Exxon Valdez* saga with Gulf residents in an effort to help them avoid the mistakes we made in Alaska—mistakes for which we are still paying. I hoped to work in solidarity with communities to help counter the inevitable "official" story. Because correcting the false story is the first step toward accountability. It's the only way to make BP pay and to avoid the secondary disaster, euphemistically known as the "cleanup," but more accurately called a cover-up.

Underestimating Spill Volumes

It was already an uphill battle by the time I arrived. The broken pipe was spewing under a mile of ocean water. BP was the only one with access to the site and estimates of flow rate. The company's early estimates inched up as its credibility shot down. One thousand barrels a day . . . 5,000 a day . . . 25,000 a day . . . would you believe 50,000?

It was hard to tell from the video footage BP released. A high-definition, live-feed camera deployed at the leak would have ended the guesstimates, but BP resisted until Congressman Edward Markey, among others, insisted on transparency. Then it turned out that BP and the Coast Guard had been viewing HD video all along.

BP got serious about scrubbing out evidence when it released oil dispersants onto the surface of the ocean and under the water.

In early June, federal and university scientists estimated a worst-case scenario flow rate of up to 100,000 barrels daily (over four million gallons), most likely from Day One. The scientists and media then settled on an "accepted" rate of 25,000 barrels per day. (By early August, that number had been revised upward yet again to 53,000 barrels.)

Where can people vote "do not accept"? The accepted spill volume for the *Exxon Valdez* was 11 million gallons (262,000 barrels). But eyewitnesses [suggest] this was the low-end estimate. Five years after the spill, the State of Alaska released its independent analysis, putting the spill at 30 to 35 million gallons.

Underestimating spill volume is common in the oil industry because stiff penalties are based on volume spilled: $1,100 per barrel under normal circumstances. If BP is found guilty of gross negligence for failing to repair the damaged blowout preventer, fines rise to $4,300 per barrel. By the time the Macondo was capped, estimates ranged from 100 million to 200 million gallons of oil blown into the Gulf. That's a big enough discrepancy for BP to save billions with fuzzy videos.

Ignoring Oil Threats Under the Water

BP got serious about scrubbing out evidence when it released oil dispersants onto the surface of the ocean and under the water. Dispersants are industrial solvents designed to break up oil slicks into droplets that sink and spread out. In other words, they make oil slicks, and liability, "disappear."

In late May, when surface slicks began rolling into Louisiana's coastal marsh, BP CEO Tony Hayward declared, "The oil is on the surface," a bald attempt to distract attention from the huge amount of oil lurking within the mile-deep water column. He stated that BP had found "no evidence" of the oil-dispersant plumes suspended in large masses and reported by at least three universities.

Alas for BP—and the entire Gulf ecosystem—the persistent plumes became an inconvenient truth. In July, Hugh Kaufman, a senior policy analyst at the EPA [Environmental Protection Agency], blew the whistle on the industry-government cover-up when he confirmed that nearly two million gallons of dispersant had been applied as of July 20, and 44,000 square miles of ocean were contaminated by the oil-dispersant toxic stew.

BP, and its puppet the Coast Guard, pushed cameras away from the spill, then away from beaches.

The use of dispersants amounts to an experiment of unprecedented proportion on the Gulf's wildlife and people. Dispersants were developed by the oil industry in response to public outrage when the tanker *Torrey Canyon* wrecked on England's coast in 1967. As a budding marine scientist, I researched effects of the first-generation dispersants in the mid-1970s. They were like straight kerosene: They killed everything they touched.

The oil industry went back to the drawing board and, during the next 40 years developed successive generations of less toxic dispersants. The problem is that dispersants are dangerous by nature. They are solvents, which means they can dissolve oil, grease, and rubber. Workers on the *Vessels of Opportunity* (the lemons-into-lemonade name given to BP's cleanup fleet) have told me that their hard rubber impellors are falling apart and need frequent replacement; divers say they have had to replace the soft rubber o-rings on their gear after dives in the Gulf.

Keeping Cameras Away from the Site

Unfortunately, replacement is not an option for the Gulf's once plentiful denizens—the dolphins, sea turtles, whales, fish, birds, and manatees that make the place home. In May and June, I frequently heard about sightings of dying wildlife or distressed animals fleeing into coastal areas. The first reports came from the offshore cleanup workers and pilots who discovered carcasses concentrated by rip currents, and windrows of dead dolphins, turtles, and birds "too numerous to count" on barrier islands.

Such evidence is rare because BP, and its puppet the Coast Guard, pushed cameras away from the spill, then away from beaches. On June 2, I was flying on a charter from New Orleans to Orange Beach, Alabama, when the straight orange lines delineating FAA's [Federal Aviation Administration] flight restriction zone jumped onshore to include Alabama's beaches. The shocked pilot shook his head and said, "There's only one reason for that: BP doesn't want cameras on the beaches."

The situation reached a new low when the Coast Guard ignored the First Amendment and said anyone who got within 65 feet of response operations without government permission could face felony charges and up to $40,000 in fines. That policy, and other unwritten forms of censorship, have been aggressively enforced by BP's private security teams and local police who commonly work off-duty (in their uniforms) for BP.

Retired Coast Guard Admiral Thad Allen, the person alleg-edly in charge of the cleanup, said the restrictions were in-tended to protect "safety." Really? If the federal government or BP were so concerned about safety, then maybe any of the four agencies—EPA, OSHA [Occupational Safety and Health Administration], NIOSH [National Institute for Occupational Safety and Health], or the Coast Guard—that are supposedly sampling air and water quality should design better monitor-ing programs. None of those agencies has found unsafe levels of oil or the notorious human health hazard, 2-butoxyethanol, a primary ingredient in one of the dispersants (the ironically named "Corexit") dumped into the Gulf. But plenty of other people have discovered dangerous chemical levels in the envi-ronment.

For example, about a week after the oil started coming ashore in Alabama, the Mobile television station WKRG took samples of water and sand from Orange Beach, Gulf Shores, Katrina Key, and Dauphin Island. The test was nothing fancy. The on-air reporter simply dipped a jar into the ocean and another into some surf water filling a sand pit dug by a small child. In the samples, oil was not visible in the water or the sand, but the chemist who analyzed them reported astonish-ingly high levels of oil ranging from 16 to 221 parts per mil-lion (ppm).

Except for the Dauphin Island sample—that one exploded in the lab. The chemist thought maybe the exploding sample contained methane or 2-butoxyethanol.

Toxic Effects of Oil and Dispersants

These levels of oil could explain the bouts of skin rashes I heard about from coastal residents, pharmacists, and medical doctors in Louisiana, Mississippi, Alabama, and Florida. The rashes ranged from a fiery red discoloration to deep blistering. The worst cases I saw were on the legs of offshore cleanup workers who were diagnosed by BP with "staph infections." Sick workers who sought out independent doctors were fired, according to the workers.

Toxicologists and medical doctors told me that oil alone would not cause deep blisters and scarring—but dispersants could. There is also evidence of dangerous levels of oil in the air. What people described as "invisible jellyfish" in the water became "stinging rain" in the air. I suspect the sting is from the micelles, little oil bubbles wrapped in solvent. A preliminary study commissioned in mid-July by Guardians of the Gulf, a community-based nonprofit organization in Orange Beach, Alabama, found that nightly air inversions—common in the area during the summer and fall—were trapping pollutants near the ground. Total Volatile Organic Compounds (VOCs)—including the carcinogen benzene, and oil vapors—reached 85 to 108 parts per million at 9:00 a.m. but rapidly dropped to zero (or non-detectable) within half an hour as the sun burned through the inversion layer. This would help explain why the EPA has failed to detect VOCs with its own tests: The agency typically does its sampling during the daytime.

The high VOC levels could explain the bout of respiratory problems, dizziness, nausea, sore throats, headaches, and ear bleeds I've heard about from residents and health professionals from Houma, Louisiana, to Apalachicola, Florida. Even the oil industry knows that these chemicals are unsafe. As long ago as 1948, the American Petroleum Institute confirmed that "the only absolutely safe concentration for benzene is zero."

BP has consistently informed cleanup workers that wearing respirators will result in job termination.

And yet throughout the entire debacle, the regulators with OSHA have refused to require respirators for offshore cleanup workers, arguably the most at risk from high exposure levels of oil-dispersant contaminants. Under public pressure, OSHA finally insisted respirators be provided to offshore workers (only), yet the agency well knows that BP has consistently informed cleanup workers that wearing respirators will result in job termination. Why would BP be opposed to such an easy and cheap worker protection measure? For the same reason the company chases cameras off the sand—it doesn't want to look bad. Workers wearing respirators would be an admission that something is terribly wrong, and leave BP open to long-term medical surveillance.

Reclaiming Democracy

What will become of the Gulf? If the experience of Alaska's Prince William Sound is any indicator, the future will be grim. Holes will appear where once things were solid. There will be holes in the Gulf's ecosystem when the 2010 class of young sea life fails to return as adults, just as in Alaska, where the Prince William Sound herring fishery still remains closed. There will be holes in Gulf communities as depression crimps lives and families leave, just like what happened in my town of Cordova. There will be holes when the false economy propped up by BP's cash crashes to the reality that this tragedy has stolen much of the Gulf's economic foundation.

Perhaps the biggest hole, the worst wound, is the damage done to our democracy. The BP blowout and the government's lame response have made clear once again that in this country the corporations lead . . . and the politicians follow.

Accountability was something we failed to achieve in Alaska. It took me almost 20 years—and a lot of personal growth—to fully understand why. Over time, I began to see that Exxon's oil spill wasn't an environmental disaster; it was, instead, a democracy disaster. Exxon's collusion with the government then, like BP's today, made it blatantly obvious that "We the People" have lost control of our Republic. When government decides that bowing to the needs of companies is its top priority, disasters that come at the public expense are the natural result.

This was true before, but in the wake of the Gulf spill it's plain for everyone to see. As one of my new friends in the Gulf put it: "This is not new. This is just in our faces." The righteous anger in that statement might yet be able to mend the holes in our democracy. It might give us the chance to put our political divides aside and work together to reclaim government of, for, and by the people.

12

The Oil Spill Should Teach America to Break Its Addiction to Fossil Fuel

Robert Zevin

*Robert Zevin is a pioneer in creating socially conscious invest-
ment firms, including his current company, Zevin Asset Management. He is also a committed activist and has participated in
the development of other social change organizations.*

*America is addicted to oil, and few are willing to do anything to
break the addiction. It is much easier to follow the status quo
and consume more and more oil instead of buying fuel-efficient
cars, saving electricity, and advocating for alternative energies.
Oil costs the nation billions in defense, transportation, and
health expenses, but Americans do not seem to mind. Nothing
will change unless the people demand an end to oil addiction,
and perhaps the British Petroleum (BP) oil spill in the Gulf of
Mexico will finally alert the country to the hazards and costs of
this terrible dependency.*

Corrupt regulatory oversight, cutting corners to save costs,
plus citizens and politicians chanting "Drill, baby,
drill"—is the BP Deepwater Horizon catastrophe really any
surprise? The spill in the Gulf of Mexico, the worst man-made
environmental disaster in the U.S., is a consequence of our
addiction to oil. Like an addict resorting to riskier and riskier
behavior to get a "fix", we have adopted riskier and more des-

perate measures to feed our addiction to oil such as drilling in deeper water and extracting oil from sand. Some of us have the luxury of saying we weren't completely aware of the effect of our lifestyles on the environment; certainly prior to the BP spill we could hop into our cars and drive to the store and buy cheap goods and eat strawberries during a snowstorm without seeing the images of the impact of our collective actions. In fact, it is only fairly recently that we have irrefutable data that shows the environmental and health impacts from smog, carbon dioxide and other byproducts of our oil consumption. While BP project managers who cut corners and regulators who didn't do their job are directly to blame for this spill, our collective hands are not clean. It is our addiction to oil that led to an environment in which this spill could happen.

Politicians have acted as enablers, allowing us to continue our addiction, and making it cheaper and easier to do so.

Politicians Need to Do More than Talk About Alternative Energy

In a June [2010] speech President [Barack] Obama paid lip service to reducing our dependence on oil. Starting with Richard Nixon, U.S. presidents have talked about the need to reduce our reliance on oil. The most effective way to curb our appetite for oil would be to cut the subsidies to oil companies and implement a carbon tax which would more accurately reflect the cost to society of the "collateral damage" associated with oil production. In addition, politicians should materially increase subsidies to alternative energy, and make these subsidies reliable and consistent without short-term expiration and renewal concerns. Taking these steps has always been difficult because of massive vested interests in the economic status quo. Critics of alternative energy subsidies complain that alternative energy will never be as cheap as coal, oil and natural gas, however, in the United States, no source of energy was developed without subsidies; between 1973 and 2003, the federal government spent $74 billion subsidizing nuclear power and fossil fuels; during this same timeframe renewable energy and spending on energy efficiency research received $26 billion from the federal government.

The cost of our addiction has escalated, driving us literally to the ends of the earth to uncover more.

It is easy to point the finger at politicians, to say they have not done enough to help us conquer our addiction to oil, and certainly they haven't. Politicians have acted as enablers, allowing us to continue our addiction, and making it cheaper and easier to do so. Watching Al Gore's movie, *An Inconvenient Truth* [about climate change], reading about ground water contamination from natural gas drilling, or looking at pictures of oil spills; it's easy to get angry and point fingers at the deepwater oil drillers, the natural gas drillers, or the executives at car companies that pushed SUVs. However, if Americans are asked to drive less, buy smaller cars, or turn down their thermostats, few are willing to do so.

The Costs of Oil Addiction

Over 150 million years ago, marine plants blanketed the sea floor and sedimentation created sufficient pressure to convert the unoxidized carbon into oil. Over the past 150 years oil products have fueled the fastest growth in material wellbeing in human history. Especially with the invention of the gasoline-fueled car in 1901 and the incredible mobility it provided, oil became our drug of choice. The cost of our addiction has escalated, driving us literally to the ends of the earth to uncover more.

Estimating the economic cost of our addiction is difficult; direct subsidies to oil and oil using systems are often complex and artfully concealed but estimates calculate the subsidy at around $20 per barrel of oil; but what "cost" should we add for a child who develops asthma from breathing in smog? What percent of the hundreds of billions of dollars we spend on defense is indirectly or directly a result of our oil addiction? What is the cost of the environmental damage from the BP spill and from the thousands of spills prior? We do not need to come up with an absolute number to know that the true cost of the gas we fill our tanks with is much, much higher than the $3 per gallon we pay at the pump.

Breaking the Addiction

The first step for addicts going through a recovery program is to admit that they are powerless over the substance they are addicted to and their lives have become unmanageable as a result of their addiction. We can talk objectively about the problems we face as a result of our oil addiction, but without the realization that our lives have become unmanageable we cannot begin the process of recovery. We are engaged in a counterproductive war in Iraq whose real purpose is apparently to control more oil, we are facing increasing global warming, and we are assaulted by an immense environmental disaster with far-reaching ecological implications. Our lives have become unmanageable.

After this first step we need to begin to take concrete action to break our addiction. There is no shortage of energy in the world beyond oil, gas and coal. From the sun and the wind to biomass, geothermal and ocean currents, energy and the means to capture it exist; what we lack is the infrastructure and scale to support the economics of alternatives. We need to demand change. Automakers made SUVs because consumers wanted them. Ask for (and buy) hybrid cars, electric cars and fuel-efficient vehicles and the auto industry will make them. Conserve energy. Realize the implications of driving a few blocks and change ingrained habits. Speak up—tell lawmakers you do not want cheap gas, you want money spent on viable alternatives and efficiency improvements. The BP spill is no longer front page news and now we are left with a choice: move this disaster to the back of our minds and continue on as before, albeit slightly wiser about the negative consequences of our addiction, or choose to let the BP spill be the proverbial "hitting bottom" that propels us to finally break our addiction to oil.

Organizations to Contact

The editors have compiled the following list of organizations concerned with the issues debated in this book. The descriptions are derived from materials provided by the organizations. All have publications or information available for interested readers. The list was compiled on the date of publication of the present volume; the information provided here may change. Be aware that many organizations take several weeks or longer to respond to inquiries, so allow as much time as possible.

American Enterprise Institute (AEI)
1150 Seventeenth St. NW, Washington, DC   20036
(202) 862-5800 • fax (202) 862-7177
website: www.aei.org

A nonpartisan public policy institute, AEI sponsors government, politics, economics and social welfare research and publishes reports in an effort to promote the expansion of liberty, increases in individual opportunity, and the strengthening of free enterprise. With regard to energy policy, the institute encourages the government to adopt free market policies that preserve the environment while at the same time facilitating economic growth. Generally, the organization has been supportive of offshore drilling as a means to meet America's oil and energy needs and urged the government to measure its response to the Gulf oil spill. The AEI website and the bimonthly magazine *The American* contain additional articles explaining the need for offshore drilling.

Association for the Study of Peak Oil & Gas-USA (ASPO-USA)
P.O. Box 21624, Denver, CO   80221
877-363-2776 • fax (303) 451-7567
website: www.aspousa.org

ASPO-USA is a non-profit organization dedicated to ensuring that America tackles the challenge of peak oil through energy management, community transformation and cooperative initiatives. The association combines careful analysis of existing research with public education initiatives to inform consumers about actions they can take to ensure that the depletion of oil does not have lasting, negative impacts on the environment, culture, and the economy. ASPO-USA publishes periodic reviews of global situations impacting oil production, all of which are available on the organization's website, along with multimedia files of conference proceedings and presentations about peak oil.

British Petroleum (BP)
Warrenville Offices, Americas Business Service Center
Customer Service, Warrenville, IL   60555
(800) 333-3991
e-mail: bpconsum@bp.com
website: www.bp.com

One of the largest international oil companies, BP operates in over 100 countries worldwide providing oil and gasoline to the global population. Most of its gas stations bear the BP name; however, BP owned stations include Arco and ampm in the United States, Aral in Germany, and Castrol oil. BP was leasing the Deepwater Horizon oil rig in the Gulf of Mexico when it exploded and has been in charge of efforts to stop the spillage and ensure that the oil that did leak is cleaned up properly. Information about BP's response to the Gulf spill can be found on the company's website, which includes an overview of the event, videos, pictures, maps, and additional information about the incident.

Cato Institute
1000 Massachusetts Ave. NW, Washington, DC   20001-5403
(202) 842-0200 • fax (202) 842-3490
website: www.cato.org

Cato is a libertarian organization dedicated to the promotion of individual liberty, limited government, and free markets. As such, Cato scholars have called for drilling in the waters off the American coast to meet the ever-increasing US demand for oil. In response to the Gulf oil spill, Cato's fellows worried that the accident would do more to discourage continued exploration of offshore drilling options and result in increased regulatory measures that would do little to address the root problems that caused the spill to occur. Articles such as "Gulf Oil Spill: Same Old Arguments," "The Gulf Spill and Compensation for Disaster Victims," and "The Gulf Spill, the Financial Crisis, and Government Failure," all examine different aspects of the Gulf spill and the government's response.

Environmental Protection Agency (EPA)
Ariel Rios Building, 1200 Pennsylvania Ave. NW
Washington, DC   20460
(202) 272-0167
website: www.epa.gov

The EPA is the government agency designated to ensure that both human and environmental health in the United States are protected and preserved. With regional and specialized offices nationwide, the agency works within local spheres to influence and promote positive environmental stewardship and policies. The EPA focuses on specific issues such as water, air, climate, waste and pollution, green living, human health, ecosystems, and more. The EPA conducted numerous tests following the BP oil spill, monitored conditions, and assessed the dispersants used to try to help clean the waters where the spill occurred. Information about the results of these tests can be found on the EPA website.

Greenpeace, USA
702 H St. NW, Suite 300, Washington, DC   20001
(202) 462-1177 • fax (202) 462-4507
e-mail: info@wdc.greenpeace.org
website: www.greenpeace.org

Greenpeace is an environmental organization dedicated to protecting the global environment through the use of confrontational but peaceful means that directly engage those involved in actions seen as destructive by the organization. These campaigns are undertaken in an attempt to raise awareness about environmental threats worldwide. Following the Gulf oil spill, Greenpeace published information chronicling the event on its website with a timeline, videos and images of the destruction, and information about how the next disaster could be averted.

Heritage Foundation

214 Massachusetts Ave. NE, Washington, DC   20002-4999
(202) 546-4400
website: www.heritage.org

Heritage is a conservative think tank that seeks to create and advocate for public policies that espouse the ideals of free enterprise, limited government, individual freedom, traditional American values, and a strong national defense. The organization has promoted the benefits of offshore drilling for the American people, the environment, and the economy. Following the Gulf oil spill, Heritage published a report titled "Stopping the Slick, Saving the Environment: A Framework for Response, Recovery, and Resiliency," which criticized the federal government's response to that point and encouraged it to take a more proactive approach to limiting the damage to the environment, wildlife, economy, and culture on the US gulf coast. This report and additional information about the spill can be found on Heritage's website.

National Audubon Society

225 Varick St., New York, NY   10014
(212) 979-3000
website: www.audubon.org

The National Audubon Society has been working for more than a century to conserve the natural environment and all its inhabitants in an attempt to maintain biological diversity and ensure that generations to come can enjoy its beauty. In the weeks following the initial explosions that caused the Gulf oil spill, the Audubon Society arrived in the gulf coast region to document the disaster and its clean up, and to offer assistance to those on the front lines. A video of the society's experience with the disaster can be viewed on the organization's website along with statements by society members and reports about the ongoing efforts to clean up the region.

Nature Conservancy

4245 North Fairfax Dr., Suite 100, Arlington, VA   22203-1606
(703) 841-5300
website: www.nature.org

The Nature Conservancy is an environmental organization that coordinates global conservation efforts to ensure that ecologically important lands are protected for plants, animals, and humans alike. The group's regional initiatives focus on areas such as Africa, Asia Pacific, the Caribbean, Europe, and Central, North, and South America. When the Gulf oil spill occurred, the conservancy's US offices acted and made it to the front lines of the disaster to help with the response. In the months after the disaster, the organization remained on site and continued to advocate for those in the region to ensure that clean up efforts benefit those most in need.

RestoreTheGulf.gov

(713) 323-1670
website: www.restorethegulf.gov

RestoreTheGulf.gov is the US government website dedicated to providing information about the Deepwater Horizon oil spill and the response and recovery efforts. The site contains detailed information about the ongoing plans that have been implemented to address the spill and its aftermath. Topics presented include issues concerning health and safety, fish and wildlife, and the environment.

Sierra Club

85 Second St., 2nd Floor, San Francisco, CA   94105
(415) 977-5500 • fax (415) 977-5799

e-mail: information@sierraclub.org
website: www.sierraclub.org

One of the nation's oldest environmental organizations, the Sierra Club was founded in 1892 and has been leading the fight to protect and conserve the nation's environment since that time. In the wake of the Gulf oil spill, the Sierra Club began advocacy on behalf of the individuals living in the gulf region and worked to ensure that the clean-up of the oil minimized lasting damage to the wildlife and ecosystems in the area. Reports and multimedia resources concerning the spill can be accessed on the Sierra Club website.

US Fish and Wildlife Service (USFWS)

4401 N. Fairfax Dr., Suite 340, Arlington, VA   22203
800-344-WILD
website: www.fws.gov

The USFWS is a bureau within the US Department of the Interior that works to ensure that fish, animals, and plants in the United States are protected and conserved for all to enjoy. This bureau is in charge of implementing the Natural Resource Damage Assessment and Restoration Program in response to the Deepwater Horizon oil spill. To this end, the USFWS has been overseeing efforts to minimize the damage from the spill and to assist in plans to clean the areas affected by the spill. Information about the USFWS' role following the oil spill can be found on the bureau's website, along with maps, multimedia resources, news releases, and information about how individuals can aid in the clean up.

Bibliography

Books

Tom Bower   *Oil: Money, Politics, and Power in the 21st Century.* New York: Grand Central, 2010.

William R. Freudenburg and Robert Gramling   *Blowout in the Gulf: The BP Oil Spill Disaster and the Future of Energy in America.* Cambridge, MA: MIT Press, 2011.

Miles O. Hayes   *Black Tides.* Austin: University of Texas Press, 2000.

Robert Emmet Hernan   *This Borrowed Earth: Lessons from the Fifteen Worst Environmental Disasters around the World.* New York: Palgrave Macmillan, 2010.

John Hofmeister   *Why We Hate the Oil Companies: Straight Talk from an Energy Insider.* New York: Palgrave Macmillan, 2010.

John Konrad and Tom Shroder   *Fire on the Horizon: The Untold Story of the Gulf Oil Disaster.* New York: Harper, 2011.

Peter Lehner with Bob Deans   *In Deep Water: The Anatomy of a Disaster, the Fate of the Gulf, and Ending Our Oil Addiction.* New York: The Experiment, 2010.

Peter Maass   *Crude World: The Violent Twilight of Oil.* New York: Vintage, 2009.

National Commission on the BP Deepwater Horizon Oil Spill and Offshore Drilling	*Deep Water: The Gulf Oil Disaster and the Future of Offshore Drilling.* Report to the President. Washington, DC: National Commission on the BP Deepwater Horizon Oil Spill and Offshore Drilling, January 2011.
Stanley Reed and Alison Fitzgerald	*In Too Deep: BP and the Drilling Race That Took It Down.* Hoboken, NJ: John Wiley & Sons, 2011.
Carl Safina	*A Sea in Flames: The Deepwater Horizon Oil Blowout.* New York: Crown, 2011.
Loren C. Steffy	*Drowning in Oil: BP & the Reckless Pursuit of Profit.* New York: McGraw-Hill, 2011.

Periodicals

Alejandro Balaguer	"The Black Gulf," *Americas,* September/October 2010.
Bruce Barcott	"Forlorn in the Bayou," *National Geographic,* October 2010.
Dennis Coday	"Gulf Oil Spill," *National Catholic Reporter,* June 11, 2010.
Mark Drajem and Katarzyna Klimasinska	"Cleaning up from the Cleanup," *Bloomberg Businessweek,* June 21, 2010.
Bob Dudley	"BP Is in the Gulf to Stay," *Vital Speeches of the Day,* November 2010.

Peter Elkind, David Whitford, and Doris Burke — "An Accident Waiting to Happen," *Fortune*, February 7, 2011.

Will Englund — "The Gulf, Unplugged," *National Journal*, June 5, 2010.

Al Gore — "The Crisis Comes Ashore," *New Republic*, June 10, 2010.

Mark Guarino — "Gulf Oil Spill Aftermath: Will Region Regain Lost Jobs?" *Christian Science Monitor*, September 20, 2010.

Thomas Albert Howard — "Return to Sand Island," *Commonweal*, October 8, 2010.

Joyce Jones — "Troubled Waters," *Black Enterprise*, October 2010.

Michael T. Klare — "Energy Extremism," *Progressive*, August 2010.

Naomi Klein — "A Hole in the World," *Nation*, July 12, 2010.

Mac Margolis — "Drilling Deep," *Discover*, September 2010.

Bob Marshall — "The Oil's Toll," *Field & Stream*, September 2010.

Edward L. Morse — "Deepwater Horizon," *National Interest*, November/December 2010.

New Republic — "Spillover," May 27, 2010.

Michelle Nijhuis — "Crude Awakening," *Smithsonian*, September 2010.

Stephen M. Testa	"Gulf Oil Spill: Putting a Spectacularly Sad Situation into Perspective," *Earth*, September 2010.
Evan Thomas, et al.	"Black Water Rising," *Newsweek*, June 7, 2010.
Bryan Walsh and Steven Gray	"The Meaning of the Mess," *Time*, May 17, 2010.
Julia Whitty	"Deep Secrets," *Mother Jones*, September/October 2010.
Jason Zengerle	"More Heat, Less Light," *New York*, June 28, 2010.

Index